Sleeping with a stranger...

Overwhelmed by exhaustion, Jenee allowed
the sound of her own breathing to lure her into
fantasy.

Standing near her bed was the most beautiful
man she'd ever set eyes on. She swallowed,
focusing on the sun-streaked brown hair and
turquoise eyes, the full lower lip and five-o'clock
shadow. He was big. Very big, and broad, with
lines of hard muscle visible against the black
T-shirt tucked into well-worn jeans.

Even his thighs were massive, and Jenee's
throat grew tight as her gaze skittered over his
hips, where a noticeable bulge pushed against
soft denim.

She didn't care that he was only a fantasy. She
wanted him.

Pushing the quilt off her tiny bed, Jenee pulled
her nightgown over her head and tossed it
on the floor. Then, never taking her gaze off
those exquisite eyes, she shimmied out of
her panties...and reached for the man of her
dreams.

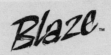

Dear Reader,

I often fall in love with my characters; well, okay, it happens every time. But Nick Madere really touched my heart. He's a big, brawny former athlete who has a unique ability, and he uses that ability to find missing children. In other words, he's a tough guy with a heart—what's not to love about that?

Jenee Vicknair would fall head over heels for Nick Madere, if she knew *who* he was, or *where* he was, or *how* he invades her dreams every night as the ultimate fantasy man. She knows that she didn't make this guy up; her imagination is top-notch, but she's simply not *that* good. And she also knows that somehow his appearance in her bed is tied to a young girl's appearance at the shelter where she works. But finding out how they're connected isn't easy.

I hope you enjoy Nick and Jenee's story and all the stories in THE SEXTH SENSE. Stay tuned for the conclusion of the series, Nanette's story (*Live and Yearn*), in September.

Please visit my Web site, www.kelleystjohn.com, to win a fabulous New Orleans vacation giveaway, learn the latest news about my recent and upcoming releases, and drop me a line. I love hearing from readers!

Happy reading,

Kelley St. John

BED ON ARRIVAL
Kelley St. John

TORONTO • NEW YORK • LONDON
AMSTERDAM • PARIS • SYDNEY • HAMBURG
STOCKHOLM • ATHENS • TOKYO • MILAN • MADRID
PRAGUE • WARSAW • BUDAPEST • AUCKLAND

ISBN-13: 978-0-373-79413-3
ISBN-10:   0-373-79413-4

BED ON ARRIVAL

This edition published by arrangement with Harlequin Books S.A.

® and TM are trademarks of the publisher. Trademarks indicated with
® are registered in the United States Patent and Trademark Office, the
Canadian Trade Marks Office and in other countries.

www.eHarlequin.com

Printed in U.S.A.

ABOUT THE AUTHOR

Kelley St. John's previous experience as a senior writer at NASA fueled her interest in writing action-packed suspense, although she also enjoys penning steamy romances and quirky women's fiction. St. John is a two-time National Readers' Choice Award winner and was elected to the board of directors for Romance Writers of America. Visit her Web site at www.kelleystjohn.com to learn the latest news about recent and upcoming releases and to register for fabulous vacation giveaways!

Books by Kelley St. John

Don't miss any of our special offers. Write to us at the following address for information on our newest releases.

Harlequin Reader Service
U.S.: 3010 Walden Ave., P.O. Box 1325, Buffalo, NY 14269
Canadian: P.O. Box 609, Fort Erie, Ont. L2A 5X3

To Rhonda Nelson, a gifted writer and dear friend.

Introduction

THE MYSTIQUE OF the Louisiana bayou extends beyond scenic cypress swamps and wetlands, columned plantations and the notable levee. It goes beyond the scents of spicy Creole cuisine and the woeful trumpets of jazz. The true mystique of the bayou is created when these distinctive traits are combined with that which has always been, the forces of the unknown that would be expected to be found in a state shaped like a pirate's boot. In this state where things aren't always as they seem, the existence of vampires, witches and ghosts isn't merely suspected; it's assumed.

Although the Vicknair family doesn't have any experience with vampires or witches, they can wholeheartedly vouch for ghosts in the bayou. But even though they *can* prove the existence of spirits, they won't. That would give away the family secret, and their reason for fighting so hard to keep their hurricane-damaged River Road plantation standing. See, the Vicknair plantation may *look* like the other sugarcane estates on River Road, but the home doesn't merely provide refuge for the living; it's also a holding place, if you will, for the dead who've lost their way.

Six Vicknair cousins currently serve medium duty, helping spirits who have unfinished business to settle before they can venture toward the light. Nanette, Tristan, Gage, Monique, Dax and Jenee know that when a lavender-tinted envelope materializes on the infamous tea service in the plantation's sitting room, it's time to help a spirit. Their grandmother, Adeline Vicknair, may be on the other side, but she expects her assignments to be handled in a timely manner.

All of the Vicknair mediums busily juggle jobs, relationships and spirits, but Jenee Vicknair, the youngest at twenty-two, is the front-runner in multitasking. Currently completing her last semester at LSU, she's studying to achieve her degree in social work, volunteering at the Magazine Street homeless shelter, assisting Gage's and Tristan's wives, Kayla and Chantelle Vicknair, in turning the former Seven Sisters orphanage into a home for abused women and children and dealing with her frequent ghostly assignments.

Thankfully, her ghosts are usually easy to handle. They're children who want to say goodbye to their parents before they cross. Jenee always assumed her grandmother gave her the young ones because she knows how much Jenee cares for the children she helps at the shelters. But soon Jenee will be visited by a spirit that definitely isn't a child. And she'll be faced with something that no other Vicknair has experienced before—because Nick Madere *isn't* an ordinary ghost. In fact, he isn't a ghost at all.

Jenee is about to learn firsthand that the Vicknairs aren't the only Cajuns with secrets. Nick Madere also has his share.

Prologue

September 5, 2005
One week after Hurricane Katrina hit New Orleans

NICK MADERE'S BLACK suit stretched tautly across his shoulders, his broad back barely contained in the fabric. He hadn't had a reason to wear a suit in a very long time, preferring a comfortable T-shirt and jeans for his daily attire, in spite of what his boss considered appropriate apparel for a private investigator. But it didn't matter what Maurice LeBraud considered appropriate anymore. As soon as the funeral was over, Nick was leaving New Orleans. Leaving the aftermath of Katrina. Leaving his memories, his home and the photographs that he'd once cherished, photographs that now had the power to haunt him forever.

Because of his "blessing," as his mother had always termed his ability to connect with other people via their photographs, if Nick wished, he could vividly experience every detail encompassing the loss of his parents and sister to the horrific hurricane. He need only look at their photos. But Nick didn't want to know any more than he did. The police had given him the bare facts, that Luc, Amelie and Sophie Madere simply didn't have time to get out of their home after the levee broke and the waters raged in.

Nick didn't need to know any more than that.

The priest moved in front of the three caskets, but Nick's attention shifted to the gilded easel tucked in a far corner of the cathedral. The easel had been intended to display the last photo of the Madere family, taken two months ago on Sophie's eighth birthday.

Nick's throat tightened. Her eighth birthday. It seemed just yesterday that his little sister had been born, right after his twenty-first birthday, a beautiful little cherub with a head full of jet-black hair. She'd been the second child his parents had always wanted, but had given up on after years of trying. Sophie was their miracle baby, a delightful surprise, and they'd adored her immensely. So had Nick.

He swallowed thickly, remembering the photo the priest had expected him to bring. In the picture, Sophie was wearing her red birthday dress, her long black curls framing a smiling face. The heart-shaped cake she had picked out at Gambino's Bakery dominated the table, and Nick, their mother and their father were huddled around her serenading her with the birthday song. It'd been a very happy day, and the photograph from the event would undoubtedly portray his family the way Nick and everyone else attending the funeral remembered them.

But Nick hadn't brought the picture to the church. In fact, he'd hid it in his attic, along with every other photo that remained of his family, as soon as he'd learned of their fate. Hearing about it was bad enough; he didn't want to *see* the agony of their final moments too. But the temptation *was* there, the way it always was when it came to his ability. That niggling curiosity that whispered maybe the end wasn't as bad as he thought. Maybe they didn't suffer. If he simply stared at those images, then he'd know for certain.

So Nick had kept his eyes averted from the stacks of photos as he'd carried them methodically to his attic, then he'd covered them with a sheet for good measure. And when he was done, he'd packed his things, asked a neighbor to watch his house, then accepted the job in Virginia.

His mother had wanted him to take that job. *"Think of how you could use your blessing to help find those missing children,"* she'd said. But Nick hadn't wanted to leave New Orleans, hadn't wanted to be that far from the family he loved, and the city he'd called home his entire life. But now his family was gone, and although New Orleans was the only home he'd ever known, he *had* to get away. Maybe for a while. Maybe forever. Nick was smart enough to realize that he needed time to mend, time to breathe. And time to learn how to deal with his blessing—or, as Nick now thought of it, his curse.

1

SITTING WITH Chantelle and Kayla Vicknair at the circular table that occupied most of their small office in the Seven Sisters shelter, Jenee Vicknair listened to an ancient clock chime midnight while they created files for the shelter's newest arrivals. Jenee had moved into the shelter when it opened four weeks ago to fulfill the on-site staffing stipulation required by the state, so it was easy for her to work late; when she was done, she merely went to her room and slept. Chantelle and Kayla, however, usually had husbands waiting for them to return home at the end of the day, but when a woman and little girl had arrived at the shelter that evening, Kayla had decided to stay until Gage got off his shift in the E.R. and Chantelle had opted to spend the night, since Tristan was on call at the firehouse anyway.

The three of them, along with Ms. Rosa, the elderly black woman who ran the shelter, had worked for months filling out the necessary paperwork and obtaining the required licenses to open the

Seven Sisters to battered women and abused children. They'd jumped through all of the hoops to receive state funding and support from the local parish, and now their dream was becoming a reality. They'd had no trouble at all finding reputable volunteers to help staff the home during the day; after suffering through Katrina, most people in New Orleans were more than willing to help others in need. And that rekindled spirit had helped the shelter qualify to house up to ten women and children. As of tonight, they had two teens, and an eleven-year-old and her mother in their care.

The teens were sisters and had been referred to the shelter almost immediately when the doors opened last month. Fifteen and sixteen, Ellie and Chylia Lee had alternated between their actual home and foster homes for years. Each time the court had tried to reunify the family and had sent the girls back home, their father, or on occasion, their mother had used them as a punching bag whenever a drunken or drug-induced rage took over. Kayla had spoken on the girls' behalf in court and asked the judge to allow them to live at the shelter long term, until either their family could be proven unquestionably stable, or parental rights were finally terminated. The court had agreed, and Ellie and Chylia had become the first to live at the shelter.

Hannah Fosset, the eleven-year-old, had just arrived at the shelter that night with her mother,

Delores. It was their files that held Jenee, Chantelle and Kayla's attention now. Delores had called the parish hotline for battered women, and following standard protocol, Kayla had picked them up from a "safe" location.

Delores's husband had beaten the woman beyond recognition, one eye swollen shut, cheeks yellowed from old bruises, mouth split open. Oddly enough, the daughter showed no signs of physical abuse, but Jenee suspected that Hannah Fosset *had* suffered. She was too quiet, too subdued, too terrified.

Jenee wanted to help her overcome that pain, the way she'd helped Ellie and Chylia. She already saw improvement in them; they no longer flinched when spoken to, or looked ashamed of the things they couldn't control. It'd take time, lots of time, and understanding and care, but they would survive the damage of their past and move forward, the same way that Chantelle and Kayla had after being sexually abused as children.

Jenee read through Hannah's information, what little there was, again. She didn't have much in her file as she hadn't spoken a word since arriving at the shelter. Jenee silently vowed to make that little girl's recovery her primary goal. She'd help with all of the cases, but Hannah's solemn brown eyes had touched her heart, and she wanted to see the girl smile again.

Her pulse pumped a little faster. She was finally doing what she wanted to do—helping children. She'd always been drawn to kids. Maybe it was because she saw so many child spirits when she performed her medium duties. Those tiny ghosts visited her regularly, and with each and every visit, Jenee's heart was pricked with emotion. She wasn't naive enough to think she could fix every dismal situation, but she was optimistic enough to believe that she could make a difference with some. And she'd start with the girls at the shelter.

Thanks to Kayla's vision of reopening the Seven Sisters, the orphanage she and Chantelle had grown up in, Jenee had a place to work as soon as she graduated from LSU. And she was gaining experience already, living at the shelter and performing more than her share of the daily staff duties while Kayla was in the first trimester of her pregnancy.

Kayla ate a cracker and sipped ginger ale as she reviewed the page displaying the violence wheel in Hannah Fosset's file. The wheel showed methods of physical and sexual violence, and Kayla was placing tiny checkmarks in the sections that she suspected affected the little girl. *Abusing Authority, Verbal Attacks* and *Using Loved Ones* each received a check from Kayla's pencil. Jenee was familiar with the wheel through her studies, but something about seeing its effects on such a tiny person made her look at it differently. It was no longer something to learn in school, but something very real.

"Rosa is with Hannah and her mother now," Kayla said. "Maybe Hannah will talk to Rosa. I always did."

"Do you think—" Jenee started, then her train of thought was interrupted, and she couldn't recall the end of the question. Her eyelids suddenly became *very* heavy, her view of Chantelle and Kayla became distorted, and she shook her head to try to clear it. She knew this feeling, that beckoning call to lie down, rest…and let her next spirit visit her dreams.

Each of the Vicknairs had signals for knowing when a ghostly assignment was on the way. Jenee's brother, Tristan, smelled smoke and her cousin Nanette heard thunder. Jenee, on the other hand, foresaw her spirits in a dream before their actual arrival, and she could usually tell what a spirit needed before the letter even showed up on Grandma Adeline's tea service.

"Jenee? Do you have a ghost coming?" Chantelle asked, quite aware of Jenee's personal calling card for coming spirits.

"I think so," Jenee said, both dismayed and delighted. Dismayed that she wouldn't get to finish this conversation with Kayla and Chantelle, and delighted that she'd get to help another child find his or her way to the light.

"Go on. We'll let you know if anything happens

with Hannah, or any of the others, while you're
connecting with your ghost," Chantelle said.

Kayla nodded her head toward the door as she
withdrew another cracker from the box. "Go on. We
both understand ghosts take priority."

"Thanks." Jenee made her way through the
shelter to the small bedroom she'd called her own
for the past four weeks.

Growing more and more lethargic with every
movement, she barely found the strength to
change out of her clothes and into a nightgown
before crawling into bed. Finally, Jenee closed
her eyes in relief and waited for the ghost. This
one was practically forcing her to sleep, she could
feel the child's urgent need to connect with her.
Obviously, this spirit was incredibly strong, and
extremely ravenous.

Ravenous? That wasn't the way she'd typically
describe a spirit trying to reach her, but she couldn't
deny that an intense hunger for *something* reso-
nated from this ghost.

Anxious to find out what the ghost needed so desperately, she let her mind drift to sleep, but instead of
immediately seeing a ghost within her dreams, Jenee
was overwhelmed by another sudden wave of exhaustion that drew her deeper into unconsciousness.

In the recesses of her mind, she knew that she
should be tending to the child spirit that had
summoned her to bed, but the sound of her own

breathing lulled her away from a basic dream state…and into fantasy. That had to be it, because she'd never dreamed anything remotely near the vision she saw now.

And it *was* a vision, rather than a ghost. Because the ghosts that visited her in her dreams were always—always—children. And the male standing near her bed definitely wasn't a child.

Have mercy, he was so *not* a child. What was going on? How had he gotten there? And was there any way that he might…stay?

She swallowed, focusing on the sun-streaked brown hair and turquoise eyes, full lower lip and five o'clock shadow. And he was big. Very big, and broad, with lines of hard muscle visible against the black T-shirt tucked into well-worn jeans.

Even his thighs were massive, and Jenee's throat grew tight as her gaze skittered across the center of his hips, where a noticeable bulge pushed against the soft denim.

It wasn't a child spirit that had summoned her to bed. It wasn't a spirit at all. Obviously, she'd been even more sexually deprived than she'd realized, willing her body to sleep so she could conjure up the ultimate fantasy man.

For the past year, she'd been so focused on her studies, and the shelter, and her medium duties, that she hadn't had time for men. Hadn't had time for sex. And right now, looking at the one she'd created in her mind, she didn't care that he was only a fantasy. She wanted him.

The sudden dampness of her panties was evidence of how much and—dream or not—she was going to have him.

Pushing the quilt off her tiny bed, Jenee pulled her nightgown over her head and tossed it to the floor. Then, never taking her gaze off those exquisite turquoise eyes, she shimmied out of her panties, tossed them on top of the gown and reached for her fantasy man.

NICK KNEW this was wrong. He knew it with every fiber of his being, but he had no idea how he could stop what was happening.

What *was* happening?

Five minutes ago, he'd been in his apartment in Virginia, staring at Emma Moore's photo and trying to connect with the missing little girl, to learn where she was so he could find her before she was harmed by her kidnappers. And he *had* connected, had seen brief glimpses of the world through Emma's eyes and thought he was finally going to pinpoint the girl's location.

Then he'd ended up here, in this tiny bedroom with the most enticing woman he'd ever seen. Nick's heart thudded against his ribs and desire ricocheted through him, then zeroed in on his cock, which rose to the occasion. He stood near her bed knowing that he should will the connection to be broken, but it would have been easier to will himself to stop breathing.

She looked at him, big brown almond-shaped eyes drinking all of him in, and then she gave him a soft, sexy smile and pushed the quilt from the bed. Then she slowly removed her nightgown.

Mon dieu, she obviously thought she was dreaming.

But Nick knew better. This had happened before, after all. But the other two times when he'd been attempting to connect with a missing child and found another psychic instead, they'd simply acknowledged one another, and then broken the link.

She wasn't making any effort to speak, or to break the connection. And she apparently had no idea that he wasn't just a figment of her imagination, or that in a sense, he really was here, in her bedroom, watching her undress.

As much as his dick begged to differ, Nick couldn't take advantage of her this way. He took a deep breath.

"I'm sorry." Was he ever sorry. "I can't do this. You're not dreaming, *chère.*"

Nick expected her to scream, or to call for help, or—hell—tell him that she was a psychic too, and why didn't they have a little fun as long as they'd both ended up in the same place.

Like he'd get that lucky.

But she didn't scream, or yell for help, or converse with him at all. Instead, she lay back against her pillow, lifted her hips—and slid her black lace panties down her legs. They dropped to the floor at the same moment that Nick dropped his reservations. She wanted him, and *mon dieu,* he wanted her.

He pulled his T-shirt over his head and tossed it to the floor, following suit with his jeans. Then he moved his hands to the waistband of his boxers and waited. This was her chance to stop him, to send him back to where he came from and away from…wherever they were.

"Tell me no, *chère.* If you don't want *everything,* tell me no. *Now.*"

She reached for him, and Nick stepped closer to the bed, allowing her trembling hands to gently move his fingers from his waist so she could take over. Lifting the top edge of his underwear, she moved the band over the head of his penis, then slid the boxers to the floor while she boldly eyed his erection, and while Nick's cock twitched in anticipation.

Then that sweet mouth kissed the tip, her moist lips opening to take him in, her tongue circling the engorged ridge, and Nick hissed in a ragged breath. He was twenty-nine, knocking on the door of thirty, yet right now he felt like an inexperienced teen, her snug mouth nearly taking him past the breaking point with one hot, delicious stroke.

Nick moved his hands to the bounty of long, brunette waves tumbling wildly past her shoulders and gently eased her mouth from his length. "Easy, *chère.* You're doing something magical down there, and I don't want this to end too quick."

She didn't respond, and Nick got the strangest sensation that she hadn't heard him at all, that she had no idea he'd said a word.

"Chère?" he questioned, and again, she merely looked at him, then eased back to the bed and pulled him on top of her.

Okay, she couldn't hear him, which shouldn't surprise him; the other two times he'd connected with psychics, they hadn't responded verbally, either. Apparently that was something he couldn't control. But in any case, she obviously understood what he wanted.

Nick knew he should analyze why he'd ended up here, how he'd found her, who she was, but at the moment, figuring out the reason behind this encounter wasn't exactly the top priority on his list of things to do. She was nudging her hot, wet center against his thigh and writhing as though she couldn't get him inside of her fast enough, and Nick wasn't about to deny her what she wanted. But he also wasn't going to be with this woman without making certain she was equally satisfied.

He rolled off her and she frowned her frustration, her brows dipping downward with the action. Then she eased one leg over his thigh and arched against him, pressing the moistness between her legs against his cock.

She moved one hand to his neck and tunneled her fingers into the hair at his nape. "Please," she mouthed.

He couldn't communicate with her verbally, so he'd have to make her understand without words. And the first thing he wanted to *tell* her was that he wasn't entering her until she came…at least once.

He moved his mouth to hers and gently scraped her lower lip with his teeth. Her nipples instantly budded into hard points against his chest, and Nick was aroused by her natural response. How many other sensitive spots did she have, and how much fun would he have trying to find them?

She opened her mouth in anticipation of his kiss, and Nick took advantage, sliding his tongue inside and stroking her in the same fluid manner that he'd soon stroke her womanly center. Her hips mimicked the actions of his tongue, undulating against his cock and damn nearly driving him over the edge. But Nick was a patient lover, and he also wasn't going to waste this night with the fantasy woman by losing control. He didn't know if he'd ever connect with her again, and if he didn't, then he wanted to make sure she remembered everything about this night. Even if she thought he was part of a dream, then he'd make certain it was the hottest dream she'd ever have.

His lips cruised along her jaw toward her ear, then he sucked the tender lobe into his mouth and nibbled it while she squirmed…and while her hands busied themselves with his manhood, one stroking his length and the other massaging his balls. Nick growled his approval as he eased along the column of her neck nipping her lightly as he made his way to her breasts. He cupped one small globe and circled his thumb over the taut nipple, then he rubbed it with his stubbled chin before slowly passing his tongue across the tip then blowing it dry.

Her entire body bucked at the sensual touch, and she released her hold on his cock, moved her hands to his face and twisted to offer the other nipple for the same sweet torture.

Nick laughed at her eagerness, and again, at her responsiveness. Never had he met a woman who was so affected by the slightest touch. It mesmerized him, intrigued him, intoxicated him. He wanted to touch her everywhere, just to see what would happen when he did.

But as he paid homage to her breasts and began contemplating how he wanted to explore her belly and navel, she apparently became tired of waiting.

Placing both palms on his chest, she pushed him to his back, then climbed on top. Nick smiled at the aggressive vixen. All he'd have to do was pick her up and toss her over, and she'd be on her back. He'd sacked his share of quarterbacks in his time playing college ball at LSU, and he'd bet all of them had a good hundred pounds on this brunette beauty. But he was thoroughly enjoying being manhandled by a woman less than half his size, so he pleaded no contest to her attack.

"Okay, *chère,* I'm at your mercy. Do me as you will. But I swear, I don't care if it kills me, I'm not coming until you do," he said, knowing she couldn't hear, but not caring. He'd stated the truth.

However, once she moved her sweet center above his cock, Nick learned he had nothing to worry about. Satisfaction was her goal—her own.

She surprised him by merely resting her wetness against the tip of his dick and not making an effort to envelop him. Nick looked down his abdomen to see his cock, so close to where he wanted it, yet hovering on the brink. And then he found out why.

Moving her hand to his hard length, she eased him to the edge of her vagina, drenching the head with her juices, then sliding his penis toward her clitoris. Then she moved it against her tiny swollen nub, increasing the friction as she rubbed faster and faster, her mouth opening in a silent plea and her eyes growing heavy-lidded with the onset of her climax.

Nick watched it all with wonderment, knowing he'd never see anything more erotic than this mystery woman using him for her pleasure.

He slid his hands up her sides to her breasts and massaged the hard nipples while she continued stroking her clit. Then he felt her body tense and saw her shove her hips forward, moving her hot, convulsing opening toward his cock and taking him deep inside.

She rode him fluidly, and Nick lifted his hips to match her thrust for thrust, until her head fell back and her inner walls clamped tight around him.

Unable to last one second more, Nick closed his eyes and set his own powerful climax free.

Then he reached for her. But his hands met air.

Opening his eyes, he saw the familiar surroundings of his Virginia apartment, and Emma Moore's folder lying beside him on the bed.

"Hell," he panted, his breath and his heart still in postclimax oblivion. The connection was broken, the exquisite woman…gone. Nick scrubbed a hand down his face and wondered if he'd ever find her again—and if he'd ever learn what sound she made when she came.

2

BETWEEN HER STUDIES for her final semester and her work at the shelter, Jenee's mornings were usually jam-packed with things to do. Today was no exception, so she'd gotten up early in the hopes of visiting with Hannah Fosset before she left. Last night, the girl hadn't spoken at all, but Jenee assumed that'd been because she'd left an abusive father and then arrived at a place she'd never seen to be greeted by complete strangers. No wonder she didn't feel like communicating.

Jenee hoped that the new day would find Hannah more comfortable with her new surroundings, but, upon walking into the kitchen, she saw the little girl staring numbly at the eggs and biscuit on her plate and knew that it would take more than a night's sleep to help her feel better.

While Ellie and Chylia chatted and steadily ate everything on their plates, Hannah sat stoically beside her mother and used her shiny black hair to shield her face as she seemed to swallow back tears. Rosa was busy turning a pan of bacon on the stove, but she glanced at the small girl and then at Jenee, silently letting her know which child needed her the most.

Jenee nodded then offered Delores Fosset a soft smile. She knew that everything would eventually be okay for the woman and her daughter if Rosa and Jenee could just convince Delores to stay away from the type of man who thought effective communication involved his fists.

A ripple of anger sizzled through Jenee, but she masked it in front of the woman and the girls. Now wasn't the time for discussing the abuse. She and Rosa would deal with that privately with Delores, the way they were supposed to, and then it'd be up to Delores to heed their advice. If she would. Many women didn't, and often returned to their homes to find things worse than before. Jenee couldn't let that happen this time. She couldn't stand the thought of this tiny brown-haired girl with the big sad eyes going through more than she'd already experienced. Surely Jenee and Rosa could make Delores understand that if she returned, not only would she be in danger, so would her daughter.

"You're going to the school today, right?" Rosa asked, and Jenee could tell by her tone that she was attempting to snap Jenee out of her current thoughts. Apparently her expression had given her away. She'd need to work on that for the future. Maintaining her calm, in spite of the evidence of abuse that she'd often likely witness, was important for a social worker. Rosa knew that—she had helped children most of her life—and she was obviously going to help Jenee remember it too. Thank goodness. The Vicknairs were all born with an extra dose of spirit and spunk, or so Grandma Adeline had always said, and Jenee was no exception. Case in point, if she ever got her hands on the throat of the man who'd beaten Delores and scared Hannah, she'd find it nearly impossible to fight the urge to *squeeze*.

Rosa cleared her throat and repeated, "You do have an appointment at the school this morning, right?"

Jenee's fists had involuntarily clenched at her sides, and she released her fingers to allow the blood to circulate. Then she smiled at the elderly lady still working on the pan filled with bacon, while reminding Jenee to control her emotions. Oh, yes, Rosa would be a good role model, and a good means of helping her control all of that Vicknair spirit. "Yes, I've got an appointment in half an hour to meet with the principal at Chalmette High. Thanks for reminding me."

Ellie's and Chylia's heads popped up, their eyes alight with interest.

"Will you get our schedules today? I'm wanting to take art," Ellie said.

"I'm getting the basic information for enrollment today," Jenee answered. "But I'll see what I can find out about art classes. And I'll also see if you can tour the school prior to the first day, so you won't have trouble finding your way."

Ellie and Chylia started chatting about everything they hated about their last schools, and how they were hoping that this one would be better. Jenee suspected it'd be much better, simply because they should stay at this one for a while. Their records showed the two girls had attended schools in six different parishes, due to their father's continual loss of employment.

Hannah looked at the teens, and Jenee noticed her chin quivering, then her eyes spilled over with tears. Delores wrapped an arm protectively around her daughter. "You don't have to worry about school right now," she told Hannah. "The summer has just started, and we'll have everything back in order well before time for school to start." She bit her lower lip, then added, "It'll be okay."

Jenee wanted to ask what Delores meant. *What* would be okay? Was she already planning to return to her husband? Or, and Jenee hoped this was the case, would she and Hannah remain at the shelter for a while and take the necessary steps to heal the wounds from their past? The Seven Sisters had been approved for long-term care, which meant that unlike shelters that limited the time a guest could stay, they could provide a more permanent form of housing for those in need, as long as the shelter had available beds. Since they'd just opened a month ago, they had the room for Delores and Hannah to stay as long as they needed. Which would give Jenee time to help Hannah.

"I put Ellie's and Chylia's school records in there." Rosa nodded to a large envelope on the counter while she removed the bacon from the pan.

"Thanks," Jenee said as the buzzer sounded at the backdoor. Within seconds, the two volunteers scheduled for today entered the kitchen. Knowing Rosa now had plenty of help, Jenee grabbed the manila envelope and told them all goodbye. Hannah's mouth tensed as though she was going to speak, but then she looked from Jenee to her mother and remained silent.

Jenee used the time it took to drive to the high school Ellie and Chylia would attend to reflect on everything that had happened since last night, when Kayla had brought Delores and Hannah to the shelter. There was obviously more going on with Hannah than they knew, or she'd at least be talking. But until Jenee figured out how to get her to open up, or until she got more information from Delores, there wasn't much she could do. Gaining Hannah's trust would take time and effort, but Jenee vowed to one day see the girl smile.

However, the Fossets' arrival wasn't all that consumed Jenee's thoughts. She also couldn't get last night's dream off her mind. Or, more accurately, she couldn't get the compelling *man* from last night's dream off her mind. He was hands down the most magnificent male she'd ever laid eyes on, with a professional athlete's build—big and broad and muscled from head to toe. And his face. Jenee had long been aware that there were two kinds of men's faces. The face of an "older boy" and the face of an "experienced man." His was definitely, and proudly, that of a man.

Jenee jammed her foot against the brake as a red light snuck up on her in the midst of recalling the moment she'd pulled off his underwear and seen just how proudly a man he was. Have mercy. She'd never formed so perfect a man in her dreams before, and now she had to wonder if any real man could come close to the one she'd imagined in her mind.

Probably not. It was as if she'd taken Matthew McConaughey's body, Brad Pitt's eyes and Nick Lachey's smile, merged them all together and created a masterpiece.

The light turned green and she turned left to head toward the high school, while her thoughts turned back to the perfection in her dream. He'd seemed so real, and at some moments, had looked intent on telling her something, his eyes absorbing her completely, but he hadn't made a sound.

Why not? Had she not wanted him to talk in the dream? She shook her head. No, that wasn't it. She remembered distinctly wanting to hear him, especially when he came. When that big body tensed and he'd plunged deep inside, she'd wanted to hear him lose control. Shouldn't she have been able to control what a man could or couldn't do in *her* dream?

Jenee pulled into the school entrance and parked her car, but she didn't get out. Instead, she leaned her head back against the seat and tried to put her finger on what was bothering her about last night's dream. How could she have conjured up someone so vividly, someone she was certain she'd never seen before? And then there was the way she'd awakened this morning. Completely naked.

What would she have done if one of the girls from the shelter had come to her room? Jenee shook off that problem; her door had been locked, and the residents' rooms were on the opposite side of the shelter so that wouldn't have happened. But still… she'd removed her nightgown in her dream, while having sex with the stranger. Her gown—and her panties—had been tossed on the floor in the very spot where they'd fallen in her dream.

And there was the way her body felt. Sated. Deliciously satisfied. As if she'd really had amazing sex last night.

On top of that, when she'd taken her shower, she'd noticed a redness around each nipple that looked astonishingly similar to stubble burn, the type of mark she'd have received if the stunning stranger in her dream had actually rubbed his five o'clock shadow against her breasts.

Her hand drifted to her chest. Maybe she'd

rubbed herself with the sheet while she was dreaming. Yeah, that had to be it.

The door to the school opened and a woman walked out, and Jenee dropped her hand from her breast and reached for the manila envelope. Something obviously wasn't quite right about last night's dream, but she didn't have time to examine it further now. She had to find out about the school for Ellie and Chylia, then she had to head to her own classes at LSU. And tonight if she was lucky, maybe she'd dream of him again.

3

JEFF STEWART ENTERED Nick's office in full confrontation mode. "Unless you can give me a damn good reason not to, I'm sending you to Atlanta tomorrow morning, Madere."

Nick had been there all day studying the facts surrounding Emma Moore's case and trying to find the little girl. He hadn't learned anything new from his analysis, nor had he been able to connect with her for more than a few seconds at a time. And the clock on his computer informed him that it was after eight in the evening, and he'd arrived at six that morning. A long day, to say the least, and it wasn't over. And now, Jeff wanted to send him on a trip that Nick knew was useless. He really wasn't in the mood for this conversation. "She isn't in Atlanta," Nick said for at least the tenth time that day.

"Listen, I know you like to wait for leads, or hunches, or whatever the hell you want to call what usually happens when you're on a case, but you admitted today that you haven't got anything. And Emma Moore has been missing for fourteen days."

"I know exactly how long she's been gone," Nick replied coolly. He could tell Stewart the number of minutes and seconds too, if he liked. "But she isn't in Atlanta, not anymore."

"So you keep saying. But you haven't given me any indication of where she is. Standard procedure says you go to the last place she was seen, to that park in Atlanta, and check things out." For a scrawny man, Jeff pulled off formidable fairly well, and he was one of the few men Nick had ever met who didn't show any intimidation at Nick's size, or his former all-American football status. Most times, that impressed Nick. Now, however, not so much.

"Nothing has changed since I went there last week. We followed 'standard procedure' then—provided technical case assistance with the local police, analyzed and disseminated information, placed posters of her all over the park, as well as damn near all of Cobb County, performed database searches. We did everything, Jeff, and sending me back there isn't going to help. She—isn't—in—Atlanta."

Nick suddenly thought of the woman from last night, which was not a surprise, since he'd been thinking of her fairly often throughout the day. But now specifically, he wondered whether she was also psychic, and had been called in by Emma's parents to help solve the case. That had been the situation the two other times that his connection to a child had been hijacked; it was because he'd inadvertently connected to the other psychic instead. Was that what had happened with the sexy brunette? Was she also trying to find Emma?

She'd seemed unaware that he was *really* there, and unlike the other psychics he'd linked with in the past, she didn't appear to be searching for anything other than…sex. But hell, a psychic could enjoy sex just as much as the next person. Nick sure did.

He decided to find out if Jeff knew more than he was telling—perhaps even the identity of the mystery woman. "Have the Moores hired a psychic?"

Jeff's eyes widened to the point that an entire ring of white circled his blue irises. "No, and I want to know what made you ask. I haven't heard of any tips coming in. If you have something, Madere, I should know about it."

Nick shook his head. He should have realized his question might get Jeff's hopes up. "No, I haven't. I was just curious, since I know a lot of families go that route."

Jeff Stewart leaned against the door frame and pinched the bridge of his nose in exasperation. Nick knew he was frustrated; hell, Nick was frustrated too. For the past three years, since he'd taken this job after Katrina, he'd never spent more than a few days on a case before determining where the child was, or, in the case of a murdered child, the last place he or she had been alive. He simply used his "blessing," focused on the missing child's photograph and saw the world through his or her eyes. Eventually, the boy or girl would see enough, witness enough, to lead Nick directly to their location. Stewart, and Nick's other colleagues at the National Center for Missing and Exploited Children, never questioned his peculiar methods. They thought he determined the child's location by analyzing facts and prior cases, though he was certain at times they thought he was out of his mind. Then again, when he was looking through someone else's eyes, he supposed he was. Literally.

"Okay," Jeff conceded, exhaling thickly. "Okay. Say she isn't in Atlanta…"

"She isn't." Nick had only gotten glimpses from Emma, usually less than a few seconds of the world in her view before he lost contact, but he knew that what he had seen wasn't in Atlanta, or even Georgia. He'd guess Florida, or maybe…the place he'd once called home.

"Fine. Then you tell me where we should be looking. Is she dead, Nick? Is that what you think? Have we already lost her?" Jeff's agitation was palpable. He wasn't used to Nick taking this long to find a child, and truthfully, neither was Nick.

"No, I believe she's alive. I just don't know where." His hand drifted to the closed file on his desk. He wanted to open it, but not in front of Jeff— it was harder to focus with someone watching, plus he went into that whole semiconscious mode when he connected with another person. And then there was the bizarre oddity that had happened last night...

The brown-haired sex goddess.

He was glad he was behind his desk. Merely thinking of her made him hard.

He had to find Emma, and he had to find that woman too. He wasn't willing to let either of them go.

"I'll give you until tomorrow morning, Madere. If you've got a hit on Emma Moore's location by then, fine you can head that way. If not, you're back to Atlanta to see if there's anything we missed." Jeff left, slamming the door behind him, and Nick, more determined than ever to connect with Emma, opened the file again. He stared into the girl's big brown eyes, and focused on her sweet, happy smile, as she hugged her younger sister.

"Where are you, Emma? Show me."

He closed his eyes and saw the same image that he'd seen every other time, a flicker of a scene through a dirty car window, trees, with dark brown bark over thick trunks and long fingers of Spanish moss draped from the branches. No mountains. Flat land...

The vision changed. Nick saw a brick building, one-story and long, with a hedge of pink clustered flowers—roses—along one side. He hurriedly scanned it, looking for a name, for a sign. This was more than he'd seen before; he was getting closer, just a little more...

Again, the image changed. He had no idea why,

but his link with Emma had broken, as it always did. And though he was frustrated by the fact that he simply couldn't hold on to the little girl, he couldn't deny his exhilaration at realizing where his journey had taken him, standing outside of a door that he strongly suspected belonged to *her.*

There was no need to open it; he merely thought of being on the other side, and he was there, in much the same way that he darted from one vision to another when he connected with a child. But this was no child waiting on the other side of the door, and he didn't see through her eyes, thank God. He saw her through his own eyes, and she saw him.

She'd known he was coming. She sat up on the bed, and the patchwork quilt fell to her waist exposing the top of a lacy red nightie. Unlike the conservative nightgown she'd worn last night, this lingerie was obviously worn with sex in mind— with *him* in mind. She slid one tiny strap past her shoulder, then shifted slightly so the other strap joined the first at her elbows. Her breasts were suddenly bare and undeniably aroused, the cinnamon-tipped nipples taut and erect and exquisite. He instantly recalled the way they'd beaded against his tongue last night, and the way her body had shuddered when he licked them, the same way he'd lick them again, soon.

Nick pulled his shirt over his head and tossed it to the floor. There was no denying what she wanted, or what he wanted, and he wasn't going to waste precious time. He didn't know how long he could stay, or how long it'd take him to find his way back once he left. Nick didn't understand this unusual connection that seemed to be triggered by his reaching out for Emma. If no other psychics had been called in to help with the search, where did she come from?

While he undressed, she leaned back, lifting her hips and pushing the skimpy nightie, along with the quilt, to the floor. Red lace panties were her only covering as she watched Nick remove his clothes, her eyes drinking in every exposed inch. And when he freed his erection, she reached for it, mouthing, "Please."

How Nick wished he could hear the word, how he wanted to learn who she was, what she was, whether this was as real as he thought. But he hadn't been given the blessing of hearing others; he'd been given sight.

He climbed beside her on the bed, and her hands greedily moved over his chest, along his sides, squeezing him as though affirming *he* was real. He knew he wasn't with her in any way beyond his spirit, but he could feel the softness of her palms, the intensity of her touch when she grasped his hips and pulled his pelvis to hers.

"Slow down, *chère*," he attempted to say, but she didn't notice. She could hear him no more than he could hear her, and unless Nick was mistaken, his mouth hadn't moved, so she didn't even have the advantage he had of reading her lips. He would have to show her what he meant.

Her body shook with need, her panties wet and moist as she rubbed against his penis.

"Darlin', let's make this last a little longer. Let me enjoy you," Nick said, again to ears that couldn't hear.

And he was beginning to see that it didn't matter that he wanted to go slow, didn't matter that he wanted to take his time appreciating every beautiful curve, every inviting indentation. She wanted him inside of her, and she wasn't willing to wait. Then Nick noticed her tense, and glance toward the door.

Nick froze. Who was she afraid was going to come in? *Mon dieu,* was this mystery woman married? No way would he ever be with a married woman, sexy as sin or not. He lifted her left hand to check out the ring finger and found it bare. But that wasn't enough. He held up her hand and indicated the spot where a wedding band would be.

She followed his gaze, then looked at him, smiled and shook her head. Then, following his lead, she slid her palm to his left hand, twined her fingers with his and nodded toward *his* bare finger.

Nick also shook his head. She smiled again, then guided their hands to her waist, where she fingered the top of her panties and started tugging them down. Nick grinned at her eagerness, kissed her softly and took over, sliding the fabric down her smooth legs, until she kicked it to the floor and scooted closer to him, their nude bodies instantly finding warmth…and stoking the heat even higher.

Then she looked back toward the door, and Nick wondered why she was so skittish. If she wasn't worried about a husband coming in, then who? He wished he had a way to ask.

For some reason, she was apprehensive about what they were doing, or maybe about where they were doing it. Where were they anyway? Nick didn't know, and she had no way to tell him anything…beyond the fact that she felt the need to rush. Apparently, someone had the ability to interrupt them, and she didn't want to risk it, not that the intruder would see Nick anyway. Nick was all about giving the lady what she wanted, but once he did, he vowed that they'd do this again…slower. He wasn't a selfish lover, after all, though right now, she seemed to want one.

She curved against him, pulling him flush against her and taking his penis inside her hot center. She leaned her head back, her mouth opening slightly as he pushed deep inside, then she pumped her hips against his, taking her body where it wanted to go, obviously not caring that she was going to climax almost immediately.

But Nick cared. When she came, he wanted her to feel something more than the physical. He slowed the pace, slid one hand beneath her hair to the back of her neck and tilted her head so she had to look at him. "I'm going to kiss you now, *chère,* like you've never been kissed."

Though she couldn't know that he was talking, her heavy-lidded eyes focused on his lips, and he eased closer, letting her see what was going to happen as he stroked into her fluidly, tenderly, un-hurriedly. His mouth brushed against hers, and she immediately opened, wanting to intensify the kiss, to speed this up as well.

"Easy, *chère.*" Nick licked her lower lip, then slid his tongue inside, grateful that this vision allowed him to taste. Warm peppermint teased his senses, and he explored her lips, moving his tongue against her teeth, then across the roof of her mouth. She mated her tongue with his in the same, building rhythm their hips moved in below. More and more intense, stronger, faster.

Nick was getting close. He'd wanted to slow her down, but she'd brought him up to *her* speed.

Her legs wrapped around his back and she clenched them to take him even deeper inside, then her entire body stiffened against his, her rock-hard nipples pressing against his chest as she climaxed… and Nick couldn't hold back anymore. He grabbed her hips and bucked into her, knowing that if he could hear their lovemaking, the sounds of flesh on flesh, male to female, would overwhelm his senses.

He came powerfully, growling through the

forceful release. Then, though his body still bristled with spent sexual energy, he rolled onto his side and pulled her close, holding her and rubbing her back as her body also shuddered through the aftermath of her orgasm. Nick was thankful that he'd at least slowed her down enough to enjoy a real kiss, but he wanted more, so much more. But she'd gotten the best of him, caused him to give her what she wanted without letting him show her how much he had to give.

Leaning back enough to see her face, he pushed her silky hair from her eyes and smiled at her. She was exquisite, beautiful in every sense of the word, and he wanted to know everything he could about her. "Who are you, *chère?*" he asked, stroking her hair, but she just looked at him, as though willing him to speak.

"Don't leave me," she mouthed. "Stay with me."

"I will," he said, but the promise was a lie, because the moment the words had left his lips, she was gone.

4

JENEE WOKE UP naked *again*. And extremely satisfied *again*. She stretched, rolled over and looked at the door. Still locked, which she'd verified repeatedly as her dream man made love to her. She'd been so nervous that someone might try to come in, which would have been ridiculous *if* he were merely a dream.

But he wasn't. She'd realized it after he left, when she'd lain in bed wishing he'd return, still feeling the warmth of his body on her sheets and knowing without a doubt that she wasn't sleeping. She *had* been with that sexy stranger last night, but she couldn't fathom *how*. The logical reason, given she was a Vicknair medium, would be that he was a ghost stuck in the middle who had zoned in on her because of her ability. That would be logical, but it wasn't probable, for several reasons.

One, every ghost she'd ever met had eyes as black as onyx, but his were a blinding turquoise. And ghosts glowed, faintly at first, then more brilliantly as they neared their time to cross. He hadn't been glowing, though he had appeared different from the living, more dreamlike, almost ethereal, as though she was seeing through to his complete essence. And then there was the fact that they couldn't communicate. Jenee never had a problem conversing with child spirits, but he couldn't speak to her. *Why?* What kind of spirit could come to her, make wild love to her, yet not talk to her?

She held up her hand, recalling the way he'd silently asked her marital status. That had been so *adorable.* And so *not* what would have happened in a dream. If she'd dreamed him, he'd have known she was single. And if she'd dreamed him, she wouldn't still feel the effects of their lovemaking on her body. She placed her palm beneath her navel, pressed in and could almost feel the sweet, sizzling sensation of having him so far inside, sending her more-than-willing body to a climax that had her toes curling so hard her legs had cramped. She'd wrapped them around his back more for relief than anything else, and the action had driven him even farther inside of her, touched a part of her that she was certain had never been touched before.

It was amazing. It was maddening. She hadn't wanted him to go, had begged him to stay. For a moment, those turquoise eyes seemed to understand her request, and Jenee had actually thought he was going to curl up beside her and hold her forever.

Then he disappeared.

The corner of her mouth tugged down and she

climbed from beneath the covers. Still naked, she looked at her reflection in the full-length mirror on the back of the door and imagined him, standing behind her, his erection pressing against her bottom and his muscled arms circling her, touching her, bringing her to another climax. He'd like that, she realized, making her come while she watched in the mirror. That was his way, slowly, gently, meaningfully. He put a lot into his lovemaking, but Jenee had rushed him, scared that one of the girls might need her and come knocking on her door. If one of them had, she'd have had to leave him, or send him away—whatever it took to help the girls. They were in her care, after all. And he was…

Well, Jenee didn't know what he was. He didn't seem to be a ghost, but he certainly didn't seem to be a normal man, either. No normal man had ever made her *feel* so much. That kiss. Have mercy, he knew how to kiss. She touched her lower lip, remembered him teasing it with his tongue, the way her body had quivered from the sensation, the intoxicating desire, that had been conveyed by that one kiss. The intimacy of it seemed to magnify everything else that had happened between them, and she'd actually whimpered from the surge of emotions that enveloped her so completely. She'd never been kissed so softly, so passionately, so lovingly…

But she didn't know this man—this spirit. How could he kiss her like that when all they'd done was have sex? It was just sex, wasn't it? Her heart sputtered in her chest as though wanting to give her a different answer than the one she'd decided was best.

"Just sex," she whispered.

"Jenee? You awake?" Chantelle's voice echoed from the other side of the door.

Jenee was glad the door was locked, or her sister-in-law might have walked in and found her staring at her naked image in the mirror, touching her lip and daydreaming about a ghost—spirit—whatever—who could nearly bring her to orgasm with his kiss. She bit back a laugh. "I'm awake. I'll be out as soon as I shower." An image of her sizable stranger joining her beneath the pulsing hot water teased her thoughts, but she didn't really think that was possible. So far, he'd only joined her in bed. She glanced back at the tiny bed, and fought the urge to climb back in and see if he'd return.

"What time is your class today?"

Nothing like a blatant reminder of reality to snap you out of your sex fantasies. "It's at noon," Jenee said, scooping up the red teddie and panties from the floor and tossing them under the sheets. She withdrew her oversize nightshirt from her dresser and slipped it on, then opened the door so Chantelle could enter her bedroom.

Chantelle moved to the doorway, but didn't come inside, apparently in a hurry to convey her information and get back to whatever she was doing.

"That's what I thought. I'm glad you've got a little time before you go. I told Rosa I'd meet with our volunteers this morning, since Tristan will be working longer at the firehouse than he expected."

"Is he at a fire now? Is everything okay?" Jenee asked, often leery of her brother's dangerous occupation. Tristan faced raging fires with an apparent lack of fear and a fierce determination to save as many lives as possible. Admirable qualities for a firefighter, but Jenee suspected—no, she knew—that her brother went above and beyond traditional firefighter duties. Maybe it was because he often helped those souls that were killed in the fires to cross over afterward, and he hated knowing he hadn't been able to save them, to keep them on this side. In any case, Jenee worried about him continually.

"There was a fire in an abandoned warehouse near Destrehan but no one was inside, and they've contained it. However, he'll be at the station a little longer than he planned this morning."

"I'm glad no one was hurt," Jenee said. And that Tristan wouldn't have to face a spirit who didn't make it out of that building.

"But since he is going to be late getting home, I told Rosa that I could stay longer this morning and help with the volunteers. She said she's going to speak to Delores Fosset and find out what options she and Hannah have for family support, if any. Rosa thought perhaps you should try to talk to

Hannah. She seemed to connect with you more than the rest of us."

"I don't know how you could tell, since she hasn't spoken at all, but I'd like to try and talk to her."

"She seemed to really focus on you when she and her mother first got here. That's as much of an interaction as I've seen, and Rosa saw it too. I think if she'd speak to anyone, it'd be you."

Jenee nodded. "I'll hurry and shower, then spend some time with her before I go to class. Is Kayla coming to the shelter? You won't be able to stay here all day, will you?"

"I actually brought my computer so I could work on my writing here if I need to, but I think Kayla will be in later. Gage called and said she's having a pretty rough time with the morning sickness right now." Chantelle sighed. "I sure hope that settles down as she gets further into the pregnancy. Rosa will need her here. I'll help whenever I can, but I do need to work on my next book."

"After I graduate, I'll be able to work more hours. That's only six weeks away," Jenee added, pleased that she didn't have much longer before she could work at the shelter full-time. "And we're getting more volunteers. That should help in the interim."

"Which reminds me, I need to go talk to them. Oh, Ellie and Chylia are in the kitchen and seem to be doing fine. They asked to help clean up after breakfast. They're really sweet girls," Chantelle said. "It's a shame that their family life has been so screwed up. And Hannah is in the reading room, holding a book."

"*Holding* a book?"

Chantelle tucked a long blond curl behind her ear, then shrugged slightly. "I asked her if she wanted me to read it to her, but she shook her head. Maybe you could try."

"I'll see if I can help."

After Chantelle went to meet with the volunteers, Jenee quickly showered and dressed, then left her room with only a twinge of reluctance. As much as she needed her fantasy man, there was a little girl who needed her more. She'd return to him...later.

NICK WAS STILL pissed when he arrived at work. He'd been unable to sleep, because he couldn't stop thinking about the little girl, or the sexy brunette. Both of them had evaded him again.

He hadn't been in Emma Moore's head long enough to figure out her location, then he'd been unable to reconnect with her despite trying all night. She could be in Florida, or Louisiana, or somewhere else entirely. The vision he'd seen was definitely swampland, but hell, there was plenty of that around. And who was to say she hadn't merely passed through a swamp on her way to whatever location she was at now? The place with the long, unidentifiable brick building.

Then after losing his connection with Emma, he hadn't been able to hold on to his fantasy woman.

"Don't leave me. Stay with me."

His mind had said yes; however, his body, or spirit, or whatever had been with her in that tiny bedroom last night, had other plans.

He passed through the lobby without responding to those who greeted him good day. It wasn't a good day; it was a hellacious day already, and it had the strong potential to get worse, since Jeff Stewart was determined to send him back to Atlanta if Nick didn't latch on to a lead for Emma's location. And he would be even more adamant about sending Nick back today, since they'd officially passed the two-week mark.

The likelihood of recovery after fourteen days was low, but that wasn't why the number was significant. Jeff's own daughter had been kidnapped when she was only three; that was the reason he fought for missing children. He understood what the parents were feeling, what the families were going through, and he never, ever gave up on finding a child. His daughter, or rather her body, had been found…fifteen days after her abduction. Understandably, day fifteen of any case was hell on Jeff. Today was day fifteen of Emma Moore's case, and Nick really wanted to give Jeff good news but he didn't have any.

"Morning, Nick," a woman's voice addressed him as he passed her in the hall.

Nick grunted. That was as good as he could give at the moment. Two weeks of having no leads whatsoever in his case and finding himself unable to control his own damn fantasies had a lousy effect on his own disposition. He was tired, irritable, and—oddly enough, given the hot sex he'd had with the woman in his vision—he was horny. The image of her, naked and beckoning him to her bed, her arms reaching toward him as though she couldn't get enough, her body so incredibly hot and ready, teased his mind continually, no matter where he was or what he was doing.

Even when he focused on Emma, staring at the little girl's photo and trying to establish a connection, there was a hint of the woman's presence in the recesses of his mind. Nick had never experienced anything like it before. Typically, when he looked through another's eyes, he was completely absorbed by that person's vision. He usually had to struggle to remember who *he* was when he connected with someone else. But when he connected with Emma, he did remember. He was Nick Madere. She was Emma Moore. And the woman, the sexy brunette, was nearby, waiting a short distance away in his thoughts. Not a psychic hired to find Emma, but definitely *something* otherworldly.

Nick turned the corner and took in the familiar sight that always made his stomach involuntarily clench. Photographs of children lined both sides of the hallway ahead. Rows and rows of young faces smiled from their frames, their eyes so alight, so happy, so *alive.* That was what bothered Nick the most. These were the children that the center had successfully found, "recovered" for their families. But the positive effect of the wall, the implication that the center was winning the war against those who'd take children from their loved ones, was lost on Nick. Because "recovered" didn't mean alive, as Nick had found out, the first time he'd viewed this wall during his interview process. Recovered merely meant that the young person had been returned home; it didn't mean that he or she had been breathing at the time.

He paused beside Cassie Stewart's photo and, as usual, a tug of grief for Jeff yanked at his heart. Nick wanted Emma Moore's photo to hang on the wall, but he didn't want her to have that kind of recovery. Four children. He'd "lost" four children—three girls and one boy—since starting to work for the center. He'd recovered their bodies, due to seeing their last moments, but while that provided the closure that so many families desperately needed, it wasn't a success story. And Nick didn't want Emma to be number five on his ill-fated list.

He entered his office, fell into his chair and opened her file. Big brown eyes stared back at him, and shiny blond pigtails so pale they were nearly white framed her face. She squeezed her little sister so tightly that their grins mashed against each other and one of her pigtails pressed between their cherubic cheeks. He could almost hear their giggles echoing from the photo. She was eleven years old, the same age Sophie would've been this year, and that fact made Nick even more determined to save her. "Show me something, *chère*. Show me where you are. We're running out of time. You aren't in Atlanta. I know you aren't. But where are you?"

Nick had no sooner asked the question than he saw the world through Emma's eyes.

The room was cozy, not overly large, but big enough not to appear stuffy. An olive-green sofa was centered on one wall with square red pillows perched on each end. The window was open, its sheer cream-colored curtains barely moving as though touched with the lightest of breezes. An oblong throw rug, sprinkled with creams and greens and reds, covered the majority of the hardwood floor. There were books everywhere, along the coffee table in front of the couch and filling three old-fashioned wrought-iron baker's racks along the opposite wall. Two of the racks held books for children, and that's where his attention—Emma's attention—was focused. The image slanted sideways as she scanned the titles on the spines. Then the vision righted itself, and quickly moved from the bookshelf to the doorway.

Nick scanned the wall around the door, tried to

look for something that would tell him where Emma was. But before he identified any helpful clues, someone appeared in the doorway.

She looked very different from every other time he'd seen her, that silky brown hair pulled back in a high ponytail that draped past one shoulder. It appeared a shade lighter in the brightness of the room, and he noticed golden highlights shimmering in the rich chestnut hue. His palms tingled, wanting to rid her of the thin purple band that held her hair in place so he could watch it tumble, wild and free, the way it was when he'd seen it last. A fitted LSU T-shirt hugged her curvy breasts and accented her slim waist. Faded blue jeans with a hole just above the right knee encased toned, athletic legs. She looked vibrant and—young. But there was no doubt that this was his mystery woman; the extremely youthful appearance was undoubtedly due to her attire, the ponytail and the natural state of her features. Even without makeup, she was more exquisite than any model he'd ever seen, her high cheekbones, full lips and intense brown eyes giving her the exotic appeal that'd drawn him in two nights ago, when he'd first found himself in her bedroom.

Nick had been so certain he'd connected with Emma, but now he realized he was back at his dream girl's home. He'd never seen anything beyond her bedroom, had never seen her, in fact, when she wasn't scantily clothed, if clothed at all, and coaxing him into bed.

But she wasn't coaxing him now. In fact, she looked at him with such compassion, such affection, as though she simply wanted to help him, care for him, be close to him. Then she moved toward him, gradually approaching as though nervous, as though she hadn't been completely naked before him last night. She eased to a crouch in front of him and her mouth moved.

Nick focused on the heart-shaped lips and reached for her, intending to kiss her like he had last night. But his arms wouldn't move, and he'd been so absorbed in the thought of kissing her that he hadn't paid attention to what she'd mouthed.

The banging of his office door against the wall jerked Nick away from the vision and forced his attention on another person entirely, Jeff Stewart. His red hair was standing on end, as though he'd slept wrong, or had been up all night. Nick suspected the latter. Jeff's cheeks were also splashed with color, the way they always were when he got excited or anxious.

"Okay, you've got my attention," Nick said, closing Emma's file and hoping that Jeff's exhilaration had something to do with her case.

"We've got a lead on the Moore case," Jeff said breathlessly. "A cybertip." The cybertipline feature on missingkids.com was a key asset in helping the center recover lost children. Individuals could report sightings online with the mere click of a button, and could do so anonymously, if they chose, which most did. As long as the computer they were using had a microphone and speakers, they could actually talk to a call-center operator or they could communicate via a chat window.

"Someone saw her?"

"Yeah. She's—"

"In Florida? Or Louisiana?" Nick interrupted, too impatient to wait. If they knew where she was, they needed to go get her. Now.

Jeff's eyes widened in blatant shock. "How the hell—"

"Which one?"

"Louisiana. According to the woman on the tipline, Emma Moore was with a man and woman at a small hotel in a place called Kenner. That's just outside of—"

"Just outside of New Orleans," Nick finished. "Actually, it's about twenty minutes out, right by the airport. How soon can I leave?"

"You're on the next flight out, leaves in two hours, but there's more. She actually gave us a nice bit of evidence to work with. It's a cold lead, since the information was from almost two weeks ago, but at least it's a place to start."

Nick already had his starting point, the swamp and the brick building, but he also wanted to know what had been provided in the cybertip.

"You can walk with me to my car and brief me on the way."

By the time they got to Nick's car, Jeff had provided him with a full account of the sighting. Nick asked for a copy of the cybertip transcript, as well as the IP address for the computer used to deliver the tip. Jeff, always on top of his game, had already requested both.

Nick took advantage of the drive to the airport to absorb the details Jeff had relayed. The sighting had occurred late at night at a hotel in Kenner. The woman had stated that she was sleeping in her room when she woke to the sounds of a heated argument outside her door. Curious as to whether she should notify the front desk, she had peeked out her window and saw a man and woman facing off with a little blond girl standing between them. The girl was crying, and the woman had assumed it was because her parents were arguing. When the call-center specialist had asked if she could tell what they were arguing about, she'd replied that they were arguing over the little girl. The mother—or the woman she'd thought was the mother at the time—was saying that the girl was too young, and that she wouldn't let him send her "out there." The man had turned furious and grabbed her by the shoulders, but then two teenage girls had come out of a room and started yelling at him to calm down. The woman watching had assumed these were also the couple's children, because he seemed to listen to the girls. Then they'd all returned to the room where the teens had been, but not before the mother had jerked her head toward the spying woman. The lady knew she'd been caught and said she didn't attempt to see the bickering family again. She'd basically forgotten the incident until she returned home, went grocery shopping and noticed a photo of the same pretty little blond girl on a bulletin board for missing children.

Nick was instantly grateful that so many grocers across the country had started adhering to the center's request to place the boards in their entrances. Next to cybertips, they were their most successful way of gathering information. Thanks to that bulletin board and the woman calling in the tip, the local authorities in Kenner had already started an investigation, and Nick was on his way to the right location, rather than back to Atlanta.

He parked his car in the long-term parking lot, and grabbed the duffel bag he always kept packed in the trunk. When he'd left his apartment this morning, he had no idea where his connection with Emma would take him. Now he was headed back to the place that he'd only visited sporadically, just often enough to check on his house, since Katrina had robbed him of his family three years ago. A place he used to call home.

His mind darted to the stack of photos tucked in his attic. On every trip home during the past three years, he'd consciously stayed away from the attic, and those pictures. But lately, maybe because of Emma Moore being the same age Sophie would've been, he'd longed to see those photographs of his family again. But Nick wasn't certain he could look at them and control the urge to see their final moments, to know what they'd experienced that fatal day.

When he was a child and still trying to understand the odd blessing he'd been born with, his mother had explained that he'd inherited his ability from her ancestors; her grandmother had also had the gift. Back then, Nick hadn't realized how potentially scary his blessing could be—until he'd looked at a photo in the newspaper's obituaries and seen a man's death through his eyes.

It was horrifying but compelling to experience the moment a person died. And that compulsion was even stronger with the death of his family. If he looked at those pictures and focused on seeing what had happened on the day they died, he might learn it wasn't as bad as he feared. Or he might learn it was more horrific than he imagined.

Not this time, Nick silently vowed. If they did suffer, it'd simply be too much to bear. Instead, he'd spend his time in New Orleans focusing every ounce of his ability on finding Emma Moore.

It was fitting—Nick's blessing had driven him from New Orleans, and now, it called him back.

5

JENEE ENTERED the reading room and saw Hannah, her dark brown eyes wide and her hands clutching a small blue-and-white book against her chest. "Hi, Hannah."

She blinked, and her lower lip trembled, but she didn't speak. Then she bowed her head, once again using her black hair to shield her face.

Jenee crossed the room slowly, timidly, not wanting to scare the child. Then Hannah looked up at her again, and Jenee's entire body prickled with apprehension. She had the strangest impression that they were being watched, but that was absurd. There were no cameras in the shelter, and through the open window, she could easily see all the way down the dirt road to the deserted street. The privacy of the location had been a bonus in converting the old orphanage to a sanctuary for battered women and children. If a car started up the long, winding driveway, they'd know. But no one had arrived since the volunteers this morning. No one…

Turquoise eyes. For a fraction of a second, she envisioned those mesmerizing eyes. The little girl stiffened slightly, and Jenee knew that Hannah must have sensed her uneasiness. She forced herself to push the questioning thoughts out of her head, to stop wondering exactly what was happening with her ghost now and concentrate on what was most important, Hannah Fosset. She slowly eased down in front of her, looked into those sad dark eyes and gave her the most reassuring smile she could manage. "Okay if I stay in here with you for a little while?"

Hannah nodded, but her eyes brimmed with tears that pricked Jenee's heart. A little girl like this should never, ever be so sad.

"Are you wanting to read that book?" Jenee kept her voice at a steady, comforting cadence. "Would you like for me to read to you? I love this book."

For the tiniest of moments, Jenee thought Hannah would answer her, but she only nodded and nervously handed the book to Jenee.

Jenee hated whoever had put this much fear in the girl, presumably her father. Delores had said this wasn't the first time her husband had hit her, and she'd also said that she didn't plan to take him back again. Jenee truly hoped she would keep that promise.

She opened the book and began reading *Four Beds for Tiny,* a book about a puppy that continued to outgrow her beds. Hannah listened intently to every word and kept her attention riveted on the colorful pictures of puppy and family on every page.

When Jenee finished reading, Hannah gave her the faintest smile.

"Do you want to read another?"

A slight nod.

Jenee stood, crossed the room and found another book similar to the first. She held it up and smiled. "This one has a little girl who looks a lot like you," she said thoughtfully. She held up the book to show Hannah the cover, displaying a pretty black-haired girl jumping rope.

Hannah emitted a gasping wail. The tears that had been edging away from the surface began to pour freely down her soft cheeks, and she ran from the room.

Jenee darted after her, sprinting down the hall and nearly running right into Delores Fosset.

"What's wrong with her?" Delores asked, obviously panicked. "What happened to her? What happened to—my daughter?"

"I don't know," Jenee said, looking first to Delores and then to Rosa, standing beside Hannah's mother with concern etched plainly on her weathered face.

"Jenee, what happened?" Rosa asked, her elderly voice cracking in the middle of the last word.

"I read a book to her, and she enjoyed it. Then I picked another one—this one." She held up the book. "I said it was about a little girl who looked like her and she got upset." Jenee didn't know what to do, what to say. She hadn't done anything wrong, had she? She'd only wanted to help.

"Please don't read to her again," Delores said. "I'll go talk to her. She'll be fine. We just have—things that upset us."

Jenee and Rosa both waited for more explanation. None came. After Delores went to the room she shared with her daughter, Jenee said solemnly, "I have no idea what I did wrong."

"You didn't do anything wrong, child," Rosa consoled her. "There was no way you could know a book would be her trigger. You never know what these children have been through, and you have to do your best to try to help. Now you know about the books, and you can relate with her using something else. It's all about learning her, *chère,* and gaining her trust, letting her know that she's safe here, and that we'll take care of her and her mama."

"But the first book," Jenee said, shaking her head. "I know she liked the first one."

Rosa took the book from Jenee's hand and tsked at the cover. "Can't imagine what kind of trigger this would have been, but we'll put it away for now, don't you think?"

"Definitely," Jenee agreed, still perplexed.

She had a sudden recollection of that brief moment with Hannah in the reading room when she'd felt she was being watched, had even envisioned her dream man's turquoise eyes. What if he had been there? What if Hannah had sensed him too, and that's what really had scared her?

No. Jenee had sensed him for no more than a couple of seconds, long before Hannah had gotten upset—but how? She suddenly wondered if her handsome stranger had something to do with the little girl. He *had* first appeared on the night she and her mother had shown up at the shelter. And when Jenee tried to get closer to Hannah, she'd seen his eyes.

Jenee had no answers, but she honestly didn't believe her dream man was the cause of Hannah's withdrawal. No, it had to have something to do with that particular book. Maybe someone who'd hurt Hannah in the past used to read that story to her. Or maybe Jenee had tried to get too close too soon, and should have stopped after the first book. So many different things could be going on, and it was almost impossible to know what had upset Hannah when she wouldn't speak.

Jenee frowned. She had a spirit who wouldn't speak and who potentially had something to do with one of the children in her care, and she had a child who also refrained from speech. And despite all her training, in school and as a medium, she had no idea how to handle either of them.

"I still think she relates better to you than anyone else. Maybe you can try talking to her again after your class," Rosa said soothingly. She lifted her wrist and squinted at her watch. "Do you need to go?"

Jenee knew she should leave now, start toward New Orleans and take extra time to wind down a bit before class actually started. She was fortunate that her last course was taught at the University of New Orleans, the metropolitan campus for LSU, since the shelter was in Chalmette, not far at all from the UNO campus on Lakeshore. But she had something else—someone else—on her mind. "I've still got an hour or so."

Rosa took Jenee's hand and squeezed, then offered her an apologetic smile. "I'm going to check on Ellie and Chylia. Give Hannah a little time, then try again. Maybe after your class." She shook her silver-crowned head as she spoke. "I've worked with hurt children for most of my life, dear. It doesn't matter what they teach you in school, though that helps. Each child's different, and each one has to be handled differently. You'll learn the way to touch that little girl's heart, but it'll take time. For now, why don't you relax a while before you have to go."

Jenee nodded then watched Rosa walk slowly toward the kitchen. She probably did understand more than anyone else how disappointed Jenee was that she'd upset Hannah, but Rosa hadn't seen Hannah's pitiful face when Jenee held up that book. That face had stabbed her heart and made her even more resolute in her goal of helping Hannah move past the pain.

DELORES FOSSET SHUT the door to the room she and Hannah shared, dropped into a chair near the bed and listened to the little girl cry. She should say something to her, but what? She had no idea how to help the girl, no idea how to help herself. She missed Marcus and was scared to death that she'd never see him again. Her hand inadvertently touched her bruised cheek, and she winced. But if she did see him again, a beaten face would be the least of her worries. She'd made him angry before, plenty of times, but she'd never done anything like this.

The girl whimpered beneath the covers, and Delores swallowed hard. She'd done the right thing, she knew. This girl wasn't like the others; she was too young, too innocent. Marcus was willing to destroy all of that, because the men had requested "even younger." A sickening shiver shimmied down her spine. It was one thing to take the girls who wanted to go, another entirely to take one just because she was every sick man's dream.

Delores swallowed past her own urge to whimper. It wouldn't do any good. What would Marcus do if he found her now? And what would she do with the girl? So far, her threats had worked to maintain her silence, but eventually, she knew "Hannah" would speak, and God only knew what she'd say. Or what would happen to Delores if she did.

The girl's breathing steadied, and her cries ceased.

She'd fallen asleep, poor thing. Delores got up and crept near the bed, pulled the sheet up to cover her shoulders. It was July, hardly any reason to worry about a chill, but Delores had noticed that she always covered herself completely, creating a cocoon of sorts, perhaps to make her feel safer. She was safe here, for a while, as long as Marcus didn't find them.

Delores moved a trembling hand to her mouth. What had she done? What would she do? They'd need to leave the shelter soon. They couldn't stay here forever. And she couldn't return the girl, because she'd seen Delores. She knew her face and her name. The girl's youth had helped them so far, since the shelter had welcomed both of them, without needing identification for the child. But this facade of mother and daughter couldn't last forever, and Delores needed to determine how to take the child back where she belonged.

She sniffed loudly. She'd always wanted a little girl named Hannah.

6

NICK BOARDED the plane and settled in. He had just enough time at the gate to power up his laptop and receive Jeff's e-mail containing the cybertip transcript and computer address. As Nick had suspected, the informant hadn't used a home computer, but a public one at an Internet café. Why people didn't want to be known for helping was beyond Nick; it wasn't as though the center would accuse the woman of kidnapping the girl. Then again, police had to consider those who knew "too much" as potential suspects, so he couldn't completely blame her. But it'd have been nice to have a means of contacting her again. She'd neglected to give descriptions of the man and woman who'd been arguing at the hotel, even though the call-center specialist had asked her repeatedly, but a trained investigator like Nick might have been able to elicit more information. She did say that she was ninety percent certain the little blond girl she saw was the same one on the poster. Emma Moore.

Ninety percent was pretty damn good, particularly when the location where she'd seen Emma was in one of the states Nick had suspected, due to that swamp vision. But Louisiana had plenty of swamps, and even if she was in Kenner two weeks ago, it was likely she was in another part of the state now. The city didn't have a swamp to be seen, so the kidnappers had obviously taken her away from the suburb. Now he just had to figure out which way they went.

Nick had already stowed his computer bag beneath the seat in front of him, but he withdrew it enough to slide Emma's file out of the side pocket. He had to try again.

Making sure those around him weren't focused on the file in his hands, he eased one side open and glanced at her photo, let the smiling face and big dark eyes absorb his attention…

The swamp zoomed by in a blur of browns, greens and grays. Nick gritted his teeth and concentrated on remaining in this part of the vision, on seeing more. Hordes of trees went by, and an arm passed in front of him—in front of Emma—reaching for the lock on the car door. A thin gold band circled the wedding finger, and several pale blue veins branched across the top of the hand—a woman's hand.

The image changed, and the long, brick building came into view for a brief moment, a quick flash that immediately segued to the next vision, one that overpowered all of the others. This was the brunette, standing in the doorway of the room he'd seen earlier and wearing the LSU T-shirt. He'd lost Emma, but he'd found *her.* She moved closer, crouched before him and gave him the most tender smile…

"Excuse me, sir. You'll need to put your bag under the seat in front of you."

Nick blinked at the flight attendant, then saw that he hadn't pushed his computer bag back in place. Thankfully, Emma's file had flopped closed. He'd only needed to see her photograph to get the connection started, but he hadn't really thought about the fact that he might have been sitting there with an open case file visible in his lap. Not one of his smartest moments, but the temptation to connect with her again had been too great to ignore. And he *had* connected, had even seen a longer glimpse of the swamp this time, as well as something he hadn't seen before, the woman's arm locking the door. Probably the same woman who had been arguing outside that hotel room. Who was she? And what role did she have in the kidnapping? Recalling the vision, Nick also assimilated that the woman and Emma were in the backseat of the car; someone else was driving. The man from the hotel, he'd guess. And what about the teens that had been mentioned in the cybertip? Where were they in all of this?

So many questions, and Nick was ready for answers. But what he really wanted to know right now was why his vision had again shifted away from Emma and to the brunette. And why hadn't she acknowledged him this time? She'd acted as though she didn't recognize Nick at all.

He shook his head, thrown by so many factors that didn't add up. He knew he could get some of his questions answered if he learned the identity of the man and woman at the hotel. Jeff's e-mail had included the fact that local police had obtained the hotel's registry, but they had yet to find names to match the couple. Maybe by the time Nick arrived in New Orleans, they'd know, but he wasn't holding his breath. A couple involved in a kidnapping wouldn't use their real names.

He leaned his head back and closed his eyes as the plane taxied down the runway. He could use a little rest before he got there, but it was extremely difficult to relax in the cramped seat. Airplanes simply weren't made for big guys, and even though Nick was nearly thirty, his build hadn't changed all that much since he'd played football at LSU. He shifted in the seat, heard a grunt from the guy next to him and mumbled an apology. The man emitted a low snore, and Nick was unquestionably envious. How did that feel, to drop off that easily? Nick wouldn't know; his nights were filled with images of lost children…and a sexy brunette who'd been wearing an LSU T-shirt.

An LSU T-shirt.

Nick couldn't believe he'd overlooked that in the excitement over the lead; what were the chances that she was also in Louisiana?

The guy next to him twisted in his seat. Maybe if Nick could sleep, he wouldn't care that his elbow sporadically poked Nick's side. It wasn't as though the skinny thing could hurt him, but it was irritating as hell.

He closed his eyes again...and immediately saw her. Not Emma, nor the world through Emma's eyes, but the striking brunette. She entered her bedroom wearing the LSU T-shirt and holey jeans that he'd seen in the other vision, then she closed and locked the door. He started to move toward her, but then stopped. Every time he'd been with her had been at a rapid pace, much too fast for Nick's taste. If she didn't know he was there, he could enjoy her a little longer, before she tested his reserve and tried to see how quickly she could get what she wanted.

Well, he wanted a thing or two as well, and right now, it was to watch her undress.

With her back facing him, she stepped out of her sandals, then unfastened her jeans and pushed them to the floor. Nick realized that he'd never had the chance to truly appreciate the sensual curve of her bottom, currently accented with satin navy panties. His heart beat rapidly, and he was amazed she didn't turn around to find the source of the earsplitting sound. She pulled the purple T-shirt over her head and dropped it. Then her bra joined the growing pile of denim, cotton and satin on the floor.

As she turned toward him, she pulled the tiny purple band from her hair, and her ponytail fell free, sending long, brown waves tumbling past her shoulders. Nick knew immediately that he hadn't surprised her after all; she looked directly at him as though she'd known all along that he was there, watching, waiting.

"I need you."

He couldn't hear the words with his ears, but he heard them with his heart. Nick moved toward her and pulled her into his arms. She kissed him, a soft, experimental touch that was nothing like the demanding kisses she'd always given him before.

It didn't take Nick more than a second to realize that something had happened since he last saw her in that other room. That was one of the primary drawbacks to his visions; he never knew if what he saw was currently in progress—or a memory. Now he wondered how much time had passed and what had happened in the interim, because her body trembled against his, and her mouth was moist…and salty. Nick broke the kiss and looked into her watery eyes.

She sobbed. Nick couldn't hear it, but he could see the pain in her face, the sadness in her eyes, and feel the pull of her chest as she released her tears.

He picked her up and carried her to the bed, placed her gently on the mattress, then he lay beside her and cradled her close. He hadn't removed his clothes, and he wasn't going to. She may have thought that sex was what she needed to help her through whatever had upset her so, but what she really needed was someone who cared.

As if understanding that he wasn't going to give her more than comfort this time, she kissed his neck and snuggled close. Nick kissed the top of her silky hair, then pulled the quilt over the two of them and held her until her sobs subsided. He didn't know what had upset her, and he had no way of finding out, but he knew who could help her now…him. He let his eyes drift closed and allowed his mind and body to succumb to the blissful feeling of sleeping with her in his arms.

Nick didn't know how long they slept, but an elbow to his side caught him off guard, and he opened his eyes to see that he was no longer in her room, that the plane had landed, and the skinny guy next to him was now wide awake. He winced as though afraid Nick would deal out retribution for the intrusion.

"Sorry, man, accident. I was trying to get my bag out from under the seat."

"No problem." But Nick did have a problem. He'd left her when she'd still needed someone to hold her. Did she understand that he didn't want to leave? That he had no control over when he came to her, or when he had to go?

And would he ever figure out how to gain that control?

"You got business in town?" skinny guy asked, evidently deciding Nick was not a threat.

"Something like that," Nick said, not in the mood for casual conversation. He avoided eye contact with the guy, and with everyone else, as they deplaned and headed toward baggage claim. No eye contact typically meant no opening to communicate. Worked for Nick. He didn't want to talk; he wanted to get started in his search for Emma Moore.

Nick needed to meet with the authorities in Kenner to find out what they'd learned and to establish some local contacts. He had plenty of connections with the New Orleans police, from his old job as a private investigator, but he hadn't dealt much with Kenner back then. New Orleans had kept him busy enough without him having to venture to other districts. But this time, he needed to start in the last place Emma was sighted, so along with checking in with the police, Nick would visit the hotel where she'd been seen. His visions from a missing child occasionally increased if he went to a location where the child had recently been. It hadn't happened when he went to the small park where she'd been taken in Atlanta, but Emma may not have felt any reason to panic at that point. Or maybe Nick just couldn't connect with that particular memory. He sincerely hoped that wouldn't be the case when he got to that hotel.

7

BY THE TIME Jenee completed her class, met briefly with her instructor and then went back to the shelter, she was completely over her frustration with him for leaving. *Him.* How she wished she had a name to put with the man.

If she'd thought he'd actually *wanted* to go, she'd have probably held on to her irritation a bit longer. But he hadn't wanted to leave. He'd pulled her close as though he would hold her forever, until her tears had subsided and she came to terms with the fact that helping abused children wasn't as easy as she thought. One minute, she was finding the solace that she needed after having upset Hannah and even sleeping in his arms.

The next minute he was gone.

But this time, he'd been soothing her, his hand actually moving up and down her spine when he'd suddenly disappeared. Every other time, he'd left right after they'd made love, and consequently had left Jenee feeling like the perpetual wham-bam-thank-you-ma'am fix to his manly—ghostly?—

needs. Having a guy send her soaring sexually and then leave as though he had better things to do wasn't typically what she'd tolerate in a relationship, be it fantasy or real. Thinking that he was *forced* to leave definitely helped her feelings on the matter.

She entered the back of the shelter and immediately heard laughter. Ellie and Chylia, she surmised, since the sound was very teenish and certainly not something she'd expect to hear from Hannah. She entered the kitchen to find Gage and Kayla doing the dishes and chatting, the picture of domestic bliss in the most unlikely of places, an abuse shelter.

Jenee was grateful that her cousin and his new wife were so involved with the shelter. Everything she'd learned in school said it was important for abused children to understand that all relationships didn't turn out wrong. And Gage and Kayla's had definitely turned out right. Kayla had been a true blessing to Gage, whose playboy ways before meeting her were leading to an empty, shallow life. Now he was complete, and his life had meaning outside of the E.R. because he had Kayla. Jenee had bonded with her as well; in fact, it was Kayla who had recommended Jenee for the job at the shelter, since she knew how much Jenee wanted to use her social work degree to help children. Jenee had also bonded with Chantelle, and was thrilled that her brother had finally found love. There wasn't anything Tristan wouldn't do for Chantelle; he'd even risked his life to save her from an enraged spirit.

Jenee sighed. The Vicknairs were, one by one, finding their soul mates. Monique had Ryan, Gage had Kayla, Dax had Celeste, and Tristan had Chantelle. The only two left were the youngest and oldest Vicknair cousins: Jenee and Nanette. Nanette, the oldest, wasn't interested in anything but saving the plantation and didn't have time for a man in her life, though Jenee—and the remainder of the cousins— all suspected that there was *something* going on between Nan and the parish president. Their feuding was way too close to flirting, in Jenee's opinion.

Jenee, on the other hand, was currently engrossed in sex with a nameless, nonverbal ghost. Life had certainly thrown her a curve, albeit a sexy curve with intoxicating turquoise eyes and a bedside manner that would rival the best of doctors.

And speaking of doctors, her cousin had apparently heard her sigh over the sound of running water and clanging dishes. He looked at her and smiled, and Kayla's gaze followed his to settle on Jenee.

"Jenee, I didn't hear you come in. How are you?" Kayla asked. "Rosa told me you had a rough morning."

She should have realized that Rosa would tell them that Hannah had withdrawn from Jenee's first real attempt to gain her trust. It was something Jenee had been trained for, but even knowing that was the

typical initial reaction for abused children hadn't
made it any less discouraging.

But what Rosa didn't know, and what Jenee
wouldn't say, was that she hadn't been dealing with
it alone—she'd had her dream man. And though she
had believed what she needed was a hot and heated
tumble in the sheets to help her get over her disap-
pointment, he'd known better. He'd given her a
comforting touch, a reassuring smile and the knowledge that he truly cared.

More than that, he'd done it all without saying a
word.

Jenee swallowed hard. She was getting way too
used to having him around when she needed him,
not only for her sexual needs, but also for her emotional ones. Truthfully, she wanted him with her
now. In fact, she'd wanted him to return from the
moment he'd left. There was no denying that she
was beginning to feel more than lust for the man,
and she'd yet to learn his name. Or how to find him.

"Don't be so hard on yourself," Gage said, mis-
reading her silence and reminding her that they
were talking about her experience in the reading
room with Hannah, not what had happened in her
bedroom with her ghost.

Hannah, *she* was the priority now.

"I'm fine. Hannah's withdrawal is something to
be expected with everything she's been through. And
I'll help her move forward." She gave them a brief

smile. "That's my job." Jenee had spent the majority of the afternoon coming to terms with the fact that putting her education into practice in the real world wasn't always going to be easy. She'd discussed it with her instructor after class, though she couldn't give specifics, since everything about the shelter— even the location—was strictly confidential.

"Gage and I were just talking about that, how it won't always be a smooth transition for the girls. I imagine most of the time it won't. Ellie and Chylia are doing well, but a lot of that stems from the two of them being together again. I know it's hard sometimes for foster homes to take siblings, particularly if they already have several children in the home, but I also know it's tough on them to be separated. They're enjoying being together again." Kayla smiled. "It feels really good to give them a way to make that happen."

"Well, I'd say you can take the credit for making that happen," Gage said to his wife. "You were pretty amazing when you spoke to that judge about the girls coming here. He'd have been crazy not to give you what you wanted, when it was so obvious how much good you're doing." Another peal of giggles echoed from the other end of the house, and Gage gave her his trademark wink. "See, they're smiling again, because of you."

"And I'd say you're quite prejudiced. Rosa, Chantelle, Jenee and our volunteers were also a huge part of getting the girls here, and reopening the shelter," Kayla replied, though she was practically beaming, and it wasn't merely her pregnancy glow. It was obvious that she did feel great about Ellie and Chylia, and Jenee knew it was with good reason. Kayla had spoken to that judge as a woman who'd been through abuse as a child and who knew how much a stable environment, a caring environment, would help the girls. And the judge had listened.

"What about Hannah and her mother? Where are they?" she asked Kayla.

"Rosa is discussing thoughts for a safety plan for the two of them with Delores. They're in the reading room now."

"And Hannah?"

Kayla placed a plate in the dishwasher, straightened and put a hand on her belly. Her pregnancy was barely showing, but she already had that natural instinct to comfort and protect the child. "She hasn't been out of her room since I got here."

Throughout the afternoon, Jenee had replayed her brief conversation with Hannah's mother in her mind. The more she thought about it, the more she thought it was odd for Delores to ask her not to read to Hannah again, when Hannah had obviously enjoyed the first book. It wasn't the reading that had disturbed her; it was something about that second story. She got the strangest impression that Delores didn't want her to figure out what it was.

"Jenee? What are you thinking?" Gage asked. Like any good doctor, he had an instinctive ability to read people—to see not only their physical pain, but emotions as well. And he'd always had a knack for reading Jenee.

"I don't want Hannah to be hurt again." Jenee kept her voice low so as not to be heard by anyone.

Kayla stopped messing with the dishes. "Did something happen to make you think she would be? Delores hasn't said anything about leaving the shelter yet, at least not to me."

"No, nothing happened. It's just a feeling." It was more than a feeling, but she couldn't put it into words, that sense of urgency, as though if she didn't figure out what had upset Hannah, she might lose the opportunity to truly help her, save her.

The same sensation that she'd had earlier in the reading room trickled over her skin again, as though her dream man were here, watching, urging her to do something to help Hannah.

Save her?

What did he have to do with the child? Jenee couldn't fight her instinct that he was in some manner connected to Hannah Fosset, and that the girl's presence in the shelter had triggered his arrival in Jenee's world.

But while her dream man's presence made Jenee feel calm, peaceful, safe, everything about Hannah's emanated fear, dread, danger.

Jenee's skin bristled. *That* was what she felt, danger. Danger directed toward that little girl. And it was not just Hannah being fearful that she'd see her mother beaten again, although that had to be bad enough. This was more, almost as potent as the sensation Jenee got when she had a ghost coming and could feel the child's frustration at not being able to find the light, not being able to complete their journey.

That was the kind of feeling Jenee got from Hannah. Something wasn't right, and she was bound and determined to figure out what it was.

"You said Delores is meeting with Rosa, right?" Jenee asked. "They're in the reading room?" The reading room, on the opposite side of the house from the room Delores shared with Hannah, and where Hannah presumably was right now, alone… and accessible.

Kayla nodded.

"What are you going to do?" Gage asked.

"It's what I'm *not* going to do," Jenee said. "I'm *not* giving up."

Without another word, she left the kitchen and silently tiptoed toward the reading room, halting a few steps shy of the door and listening. Sure enough, Delores and Rosa were in intense conversation. One of the main goals of the shelter was to provide battered women with an effective safety plan, a unique strategy to reduce the risks generated by their partner's violence and control. Formulating the safety plan took time because it took into account each woman's circumstances and that woman's abuser. Presumably, Rosa and Delores would be talking for a while.

Jenee backed up slowly, then turned and started to the other end of the shelter…and Hannah.

The door to her room was open, and Jenee peeked in. Hannah appeared to be sleeping, her silky jet-black hair tumbling over her face on the pillow. Jenee frowned. Obviously, this wasn't going to be the opportunity she'd thought, where she'd get to spend more time with the little girl and try to repair the damage from earlier, even if she still didn't know what she'd done to cause it.

She started to leave, but then heard the bed creak and turned to see Hannah lift her head from the pillow and look at her with those sad, dark eyes.

"Okay if I come sit with you for a little while?" *Please.*

One corner of Hannah's mouth twitched downward, but she nodded shyly.

Jenee entered the room, pulled a cane-back chair from the tiny desk and placed it closer to the bed, then sat down. "I wanted to tell you that I'm sorry for whatever—" She didn't get a chance to finish, and it didn't matter, Hannah wasn't listening anyway. She pulled a book from underneath the covers and held it toward Jenee.

Jenee accepted the offering, then looked down, expecting to see the book that had caused the commotion earlier. But this wasn't the same book; this was another book Jenee was familiar with, about a dog named Harry who ran away from home and had to find his way back. This book was in the shelter's reading room because it could be used to spark conversation with children who'd run away from home. The book was for younger readers, but it had still evidently captured Hannah's interest. "Do you want me to read this to you?"

Hannah didn't respond, but scooted up in the bed, apparently to listen.

Jenee read the book, but couldn't concentrate on the words. She was too focused on determining what was happening. Why had Hannah changed her mind about Jenee reading to her? Why hadn't she wanted Jenee to read the other book? And why was she in here, alone, when Ellie and Chylia were down the hall having a good time? The other girls would welcome her company, if she'd only talk— or come out of her room.

When Jenee finished, Hannah sighed, then eased back beneath the covers and settled in. Apparently, she was used to having a bedtime story. Jenee smiled. Undoubtedly all of the emotional turmoil had worn the girl out, and she looked absolutely exhausted. Sleep would do her good.

"Sweet dreams, Hannah," Jenee said, placing the

book on the bedside table. Then she put the chair back in place and turned to go.

"She doesn't."

Jenee barely heard the words; they were so softly spoken. "What, honey?"

"She doesn't look like me."

"Who?"

"The girl on that book. She doesn't."

Realization dawned. She'd compared Hannah to the cartoon drawing on the cover of that book, and for some reason that had upset her. Maybe she'd misunderstood. Jenee hadn't meant that Hannah looked like a cartoon, of course; she'd merely meant that the girl on the book had shiny black hair, cut blunt at the shoulders, like Hannah, and she'd had a sweet, heart-shaped face, also like Hannah. How was she to know that the observation would upset the little girl? Jenee felt like a fool. She should have realized that had been the trigger.

"I'm sorry about that. I shouldn't have said it."

Big, heavy tears dripped down Hannah's cheeks and settled against the pillow.

Jenee's heart ached for the girl. She looked so tiny, so helpless, so…afraid. "What can I do for you, Hannah? Do you want me to read another book to you?"

She shook her head.

"Would you like something to eat? Or to drink?"

Another shake.

Jenee took a deep breath, let it out. She knew what Hannah probably wanted. "Honey, do you want me to go get your mama? I know where she is." Rosa wouldn't mind her interrupting the safety-plan discussion if Hannah needed to see Delores.

Hannah's eyes blinked several times. "I want Mama."

"I'll be right back. She's with Rosa now," Jenee said, starting out the door.

"No!"

Hannah's panicked outcry startled Jenee. She jerked to a halt. "No?"

"No," Hannah said, vehemently shaking her head against the pillow as the tears fell even harder. "I don't want *her*." Then she turned her back to Jenee and sobbed.

"Hannah?"

She whimpered, then sniffed, and didn't look Jenee's way again.

Jenee left the room, then leaned against the wall outside. She thought about the interaction in terms of what she'd learned in school. All in all, this had been a positive encounter. Hannah had let Jenee read to her. She'd also spoken to Jenee, which was a huge step in the right direction. And Jenee had learned what upset Hannah earlier. It seemed so trivial, but she was quickly learning that nothing in an abused child's world was trivial. She'd have to keep that in mind from now on when she dealt with children, and especially when she dealt with Hannah.

She frowned, remembering her contradictory requests, asking to see Delores, and then saying she didn't want to see her. All in a matter of seconds. Was the girl blaming her mother for having to leave their home? That happened, even if the home did have an abusive parent. In a child's eyes, a bad home was sometimes better than no home at all.

Jenee's skin started to bristle, her eyes became heavy, and she felt a familiar yearning, a pull that was calling her…to bed. The connection between her and the fantasy man was undeniably strengthening. She sensed when he was watching her, as in the reading room. And now she could tell when he wanted her and was coming to her. As her bond with Hannah strengthened, so did her bond with his spirit. Now she only needed to figure out why. But first, she'd go to her room—if he wasn't already waiting for her, then he'd be there soon.

And Jenee was more than ready.

8

THE POLICE HAD NOTHING; there was nothing to be had. No indication of the woman who'd sent the cybertip, and no way of knowing which names on the hotel registry belonged to the couple that had been arguing outside their room. According to the cops, the hotel was three stories tall, with eighty rooms per floor, and had been filled to capacity for thirty days straight, which, of course, included the time period when Emma would have been there. Unfortunately, that particular hotel also seemed to be favored by those in town for a single night, perhaps a place to stay when they had a late flight and didn't want to maneuver their way from Kenner to New Orleans after dark. It was also popular with prostitutes. Maybe *that* was why the woman who'd left the cybertip didn't give more information; she had something to hide as well. Most people did.

Either way, the names registered two weeks ago were numerous, and none threw up any red flags. Though the local guys were still checking them all out, Nick didn't have a hope of them learning the identity of the caller, or the couple.

Frustrated, he exited the police station and stormed across the three lots that separated him from his rental car. It'd been the closest available parking space when he'd arrived two hours ago, and even though the afternoon had turned into evening, the bite of New Orleans in July still chomped at him with every step. Sweat gathered at the back of his neck and dampened the top of his collar. The muscles in his forehead bunched, and he felt beads of perspiration literally pushing through the pores at his temples.

Nick finally reached the rental, a black Taurus, opened the door, climbed inside and made haste cranking the thing and kicking up the air to the max. Black. Who in their right mind would have a black car in New Orleans? He'd asked for a different one when they pulled it around at the airport, but it was the last midsize available, and Nick wasn't about to even attempt to squeeze into a compact. Right now, the thing was like a damn sauna after sitting in the afternoon heat for two hours. Nick adjusted both of the vents nearest the driver's seat to aim directly at his face then closed his eyes. Even before the air-conditioning took hold and gave the man-made breeze a chill, Nick felt better. A warm breeze was better than thick air, and *mon dieu,* Louisiana had some thick air. He'd almost forgotten. Almost.

Nick squinted as the air finally cooled, reached across the seat and tugged Emma's file from his computer bag. He hadn't gotten any answers at the station, and he'd try the hotel next. But the last time that he'd connected with her, he'd held on to the vision a little longer. Who knew how far he could've gone if the skinny dweeb on the plane hadn't disturbed him? The hotel wasn't going anywhere, and he wanted to give the connection another shot. Hopefully, he'd see more.

Opening the folder, he saw Emma and her little sister, Maggie, smiling back at him. What kind of hell was Maggie going through, wondering what had happened to her big sister? She'd been in the park playing with Emma on the day of the kidnapping. From what their parents had told the local authorities in Georgia and then the center, Maggie had asked their mother for a soda, so she'd fished change from her purse and fed it into a nearby machine. Maggie had stood near her mother and picked the kind she wanted, while Emma wandered toward the swings. Becky Moore said she'd kept an eye on Emma and even told her to stay where she could see her, but then the soda machine had taken her money, she'd fished for more change, and when she looked back toward the playground her oldest daughter was gone.

Jeff Stewart was supposed to have talked with Ronald and Becky Moore this morning, to provide an update on the case and let them know about the cybertip and the lead in Louisiana. Nick hadn't spoken directly to them since he'd returned from Atlanta; Jeff typically handled communications with the families. But Jeff had informed Nick that Ronald Moore wanted to use a media blast to get the word out nationally about their daughter's disappearance, said he'd spend "whatever it takes" to find his little girl. The center had already followed all standard protocol for broadcasting Emma's disappearance; however, Nick feared that Ronald Moore might want to announce the sighting in Louisiana. Any way Nick looked at it, that was a bad idea. The last thing they needed was to let the kidnappers know that they'd placed them in the bayou; all that would do was send them running. Nick knew if he could just hold on to his connection with Emma long enough to get pertinent details on her location, he could find her, here, before the kidnappers took her somewhere else completely…or worse.

No, he wouldn't even consider losing her. She was still alive, and he'd find her that way. He had to. He looked at the happy face in the photo. "Show me more, *chère*. Help me find you."

He let his eyes drift closed and immediately saw an image he hadn't seen before, a blurry vision of a row of turquoise and orange doors dotting the side of an elongated brick building. The image expanded, and he saw stairs at both ends, but he couldn't see where they led.

"Come on, Emma. Show me where you are. Keep me there, *chère*. Where is this place?"

He studied the doors, extremely blurry now, and realized that each one had a number on its center. A hotel. Was this the hotel where the woman had seen them? Was Emma still there? Or was this another memory? He wished he had some way of knowing whether a vision was actually occurring, or whether it was a memory. That was the primary limitation to his blessing—unfortunately, there wasn't anything he could do to change it. He just had to use whatever he saw to determine whether it was in the past or present.

He was also limited by the fact that the children he connected with had no idea that Nick was seeing through their eyes. If they did, maybe they'd notice more landmarks, street signs or even calendar dates. But they didn't sense him and typically barely noticed their surroundings at all, due to their fear. This time was no different.

This particular vision grew more and more blurry, and Nick struggled to focus through the watery images evidently caused by Emma's tears. He saw cars parked outside of the rooms, then two figures bounding out of a turquoise door. They were indistinct and hazy, but he surmised that these were the teen girls the cybertip woman had seen. They wore short shirts displaying their abdomens, and navel rings glistened from their bellies. Tiny shorts completed their clothing. With the darkness of the vision and the increasing fuzziness, it was hard to tell, but they appeared not to be wearing shoes.

Emma's attention jerked away from the teens to two other people. These two stood close to her, and were easier to distinguish, in spite of the indistinct haze. A large man, about Nick's height but thick around the middle, and an average-size woman. Nick couldn't make out the faces, but he did see the man's burly fist soar through the air and connect with the woman's jaw. The vision was so fuzzy now that Nick couldn't tell where the man's body ended and the woman's began, but he distinguished enough to know that the beating continued.

Emma's tears were blurring everything in sight and the distortion increased, until Nick no longer saw the man or the woman, but merely a swirl of shapes and colors that seemed to rearrange and then take him somewhere else entirely.

He found himself standing in the small bedroom that he knew so well. Her bedroom. If she wasn't a psychic looking for Emma, then how did he always end up here when he connected with Emma?

Nick was disappointed that he hadn't been able to keep the connection with Emma going a little longer, and yet, he'd also have been disappointed if he hadn't ended up here again. Connecting with Emma had become something of a gateway to being with the sexy brunette.

She seemed to have known he was coming. She stood beside the bed completely nude and walked toward Nick as though she'd been waiting for a while. Did she sense when they would see each other? Could *she* control it?

No words were mouthed this time, as if she knew he couldn't hear and wasn't going to waste time trying to communicate. Instead, she simply closed the distance between them, drew his lips to hers and kissed him. Her mouth slid across his, her tongue easing inside while her hands frantically moved down his shirt, unbuttoning as they went, until she reached the halfway point and then ripped the sides apart, sending the last two buttons tumbling to the floor.

She turned and watched them roll across the floor. Nick imagined they were somewhat noisy on the hardwood, but he couldn't hear a thing. Then she glanced back at him, and it didn't matter that this vision was silent; her eyes were speaking volumes, silently conveying that she wanted him, burned for him, the same way that Nick burned for her.

Her hands slid over his hot skin and heat spread through him like a levee bonfire, powerful and commanding. Nick tunneled his fingers through her hair, pulled her face even closer and kissed her wildly, while her trembling hands continued their quest of getting him as naked as her. Within seconds, they were both nude and hot and sweaty, their bodies burning for more, shaking with the need to find release.

Nick wasn't attempting to slow her down this time. The look in her eyes said she was hurting for it as much as he, and he wasn't going to fight fate on this one. Slow and easy wasn't an option; she wanted hard and fast and hot, and so did Nick.

She curved her pelvis and rose up on her toes, trying to put her center against his cock, but he was so hard that it stood rigid against his stomach, and there was no way in hell she was going to reach it on her own. Nick smiled against her mouth. Her eagerness was an incredible turn-on, but as much as he'd like to tease her, he didn't know how long they had, and he wasn't about to leave without giving her what she needed, what they both needed.

He lifted her from the floor and carried her toward the bed. She looked at the tiny mattress and nodded.

"Yes," she mouthed.

Nick changed his mind. With the wild, frantic state that both of them were in, they needed something harder, stronger, rougher.

He turned away from the bed and braced his back against the wall, then he settled her core above his penis and drove her down to take every inch. Her head fell back, and Nick clamped down on her exposed neck, biting her hard as she convulsed around him, as he pumped her hips on his rigid cock. Sweat covered both of them, and Nick bit and licked and sucked the salty moisture from her throat throughout the frenzied pace, then he moved his hand to where they were joined and stroked a hard knuckle over her clit while their hips hammered together. She tensed a second time, and he pulled her slick center away from him, then pushed into her one last time as he came harder than ever before. He yelled ferociously, possessively, a warrior staking his claim…

The blast of the air on max hit his face like ice water. He was in the car, breathing hard and feeling lethargic, like he'd just had the best sex of his life and should sleep for, oh, a few days.

Nick scrubbed his hand down his face and wondered if he should be concerned that he was actually getting used to rapidly departing after sex. Obviously, that wouldn't be a quality most women would appreciate, he thought with a smirk. Then he glanced down at his shirt. The bottom two buttons were missing in action.

He smiled, thrilled with the subtle reminder that he really had been with her, that she really had been with him. Then he backed the car out of the parking space and started toward the hotel.

He steered down Veterans Boulevard, but he drove on autopilot, his mind replaying what had just transpired in that little room. *Did* his brunette beauty mind when he left as soon as he climaxed? Or was she also getting used to his hasty exits? Nick assumed she understood—prayed she understood—that if he had his way, he'd never leave.

"JENEE, ARE YOU OKAY?" The doorknob jiggled loudly as Gage tried to enter her room. Thank goodness she'd locked the door, or her cousin would walk in and find her crumpled naked on the floor.

"Yeah, I'm okay," she said, but her butt was smarting big-time. She rubbed her backside with her hand and scrambled across the floor to grab her discarded clothing. Ignoring her protesting body— how could so many things hurt at once?—she quickly dressed.

"We heard you yell," Kayla called. "And then that loud crash."

Jenee had to bite the inside of her cheek to keep from laughing. She'd wanted to yell several times throughout their frenzied lovemaking, but she hadn't. Gasped, yes. Panted, yes. Begged, oh, yes. But yelled, no. However, when her body had slammed against the floor unceremoniously with a painful thud, she'd yelled. Loudly.

What person wouldn't have? One minute, she'd been at his complete mercy, his strong hands grasping her hips as he drove into her with such force, such intensity, that she'd come twice, with barely a chance to catch her breath in the brief interim…and the next minute, he was gone and she was in midair, exactly where he'd left her.

Then everything had come crashing down. Literally.

After she double-checked her clothing to make sure everything was right side out, she rubbed her bottom again and slowly made her way to the door to unlock it.

"What happened?" Gage asked, looking around the room as though expecting to see something broken. He was probably expecting furniture, not her caboose.

"I fell down." That was the truth, though she'd had a little help from her dream man.

"Are you okay?" Kayla asked.

Jenee nodded. She was more than okay. She'd never felt so alive in her life. And wouldn't you know it, the guy who'd made her feel this way might already be dead.

Gage sighed audibly, leaned against the door frame. "I thought you might have gotten upset after going to see Hannah. I mean, I never thought you were the type to throw things, but it sounded like… well, how did you fall? Did you hurt yourself? Do you want me to take a look, see if anything's broken?"

She suppressed another strong urge to laugh. "I landed on my behind. And it's fine, thanks."

It wasn't; it hurt like hell, as did her hips from

where he'd grasped her so hard. She probably had bruises. But she wasn't about to explain sex marks to her protective older cousin.

"Well, we've got a pot of gumbo ready for dinner. Why don't you come have a bowl and tell us what happened with Hannah," Kayla said. "Ellie and Chylia have already eaten, and Rosa is still talking with Delores."

"That sounds great. I'm starved." Evidently, having mind-blowing sex and then being dropped on her ass worked up her appetite.

Jenee followed them to the kitchen, got a bowl of steaming, spicy gumbo and sat down before she confided, "Hannah let me read to her again."

"Do you think that was a good idea?" Kayla's concern was evident in her tone.

"She gave the book to me. She wanted me to," Jenee explained, then added, "and then she spoke to me."

Gage had a big spoonful of rice and gumbo headed to his mouth, but he halted its progress. "Seriously? But she hasn't spoken since she got here, right? Isn't that what you told me?" he asked Kayla.

Kayla nodded. "What did she say? Did she give you any indication about why she hasn't spoken? Do you think she was just nervous being at the shelter, or is there more to it?"

Gage grinned at his wife. "Hey, give her a chance to answer one question at a time."

Kayla blushed slightly. "Sorry, I get excited rather easily lately. Comes with the territory, I guess." She glanced toward her belly and grinned. "What did she say?"

"Not too much, but I did find out why she was so upset this afternoon. She didn't like me comparing her to the girl on the cover of that book. I thought they looked similar, since the character had hair similar to Hannah's and that same adorable heart-shaped face, but Hannah didn't think the girl looked like her at all. That's what upset her."

Kayla's smile flattened. "Doesn't seem like anything that should upset her, but I guess her emotions are so volatile right now that it doesn't take much, poor thing."

"Then she asked to see Delores, but before I could go get her, she changed her mind."

"Changed her mind?" Gage asked.

Jenee nodded. "She looked very tired though, so maybe she just didn't want to wait for me to go get her mother before she fell asleep—I don't know. But that's all she said."

"At least she's talking again," Kayla said. She blew on a steaming spoonful of gumbo before eating it gingerly.

"I hope our baby likes spicy food." Gage grinned, taking another bite.

Kayla winced. "I guess I'll find out soon enough, won't I? Anyway, it'll be much easier to help

Hannah if we can talk with her, eventually get her to open up about her feelings and all. Maybe she'll even participate in some activities with Ellie and Chylia. Both of them are anxious to get to know her better, and they really are sweet girls. I think it'd be good for them to get better acquainted, even if they are a few years older than Hannah."

"I think so too." Jenee believed that might be very good for Hannah, a couple of new friends.

They continued discussing their hopes for Hannah while Kayla polished off her bowl of gumbo and half of Gage's. Then he took their dishes to the sink, turned and clapped his hands together. "Okay, we've got to head back home. Early day tomorrow at the plantation. You're coming to the house for the workday, aren't you?"

"Yeah, I'll be there bright and early. Rosa knows we've got a lot to get done for the next inspection, and scheduled extra volunteers for tomorrow to allow all of us to help with the house."

"And try not to fall again," Gage instructed, then left with his wife.

"I'll try not to," Jenee called after him—but she feared, or perhaps she knew, that her heart already had.

9

NICK WOULD'VE SPOTTED the hotel easily, even if he hadn't been given the exact address. The three-story building stood along one corner of Veterans Boulevard, the turquoise-and-orange doors easily visible from the street. It looked identical to his vision, without the blur factor. He pulled into the hotel's parking lot and circled to find a space. The place was packed, as the police had said it normally was, and Nick thought he saw why.

Several women stood along the edge of the hotel like a colorful garland circling a tree. They wore as little as possible, scraps of gaudy clothing strategically covering the important parts and emphasized by thigh-high boots and fishnet stockings. Hell, it wasn't even dark yet, but they were out and ready.

Nick finally found a space and pulled in, then he grabbed Emma's file and climbed out of the car and leaned against the side. From his memory, he thought the argument had taken place not far from where he'd parked. He let his mind revisit the vision again and attempted to tune out the women calling to him from their perches outside their rooms.

"Hey, tall, dark, big and sexy, let's talk—" the busty blonde indicated the door behind her "—inside."

Nick shook off the request, opened the file and looked into Emma's eyes. His mind immediately went back to what he'd already seen. The orange-and-turquoise doors in the background, the teens exiting from one of the first-floor rooms, the man and woman arguing, his fist pummeling her while the image grew blurrier due to Emma's tears. This time he saw the woman's hair, an old-fashioned style, light blond or maybe gray; it was hard to tell since they were in the dark. The man was balding, his head catching the gleam of a streetlight and reflecting it into Nick's—or rather, Emma's—eyes.

The image altered to the car ride. This time, Nick saw the woman's hand cross back in front of Emma. He didn't see her face, but he did see the driver, another woman, her hair long and brown. She glanced back at them, and Nick tried to commit as many details as possible to memory. Her hair went well past her shoulders and was a shade darker than his brunette beauty's.

Nick realized that even in the midst of his vision of Emma, he was still thinking of his dream girl, comparing this woman to her. But while he definitely wanted to know the identity of his fantasy woman, right now he needed to concentrate on this brunette's identity—because *this* brunette had Emma.

Who was she? She had big, dark brown eyes and a gentle smile, not at all what Nick would expect from a kidnapper. Then again, he'd seen many a serial-killer photo where the guy looked like he could be your best friend, like he didn't have a bad bone in his body and wouldn't just as soon shoot or stab you as look at you.

Nick struggled to find some identifying feature on the woman, but saw no birthmarks, no scars, nothing extraordinary. "Damn," he muttered, and to his surprise the scene changed.

He was inside a room, but not one that he'd seen before. This one was sparsely furnished, with a double bed, a dresser, a small table and a chair. A single book was on the top of the dresser, a Bible. Behind the Bible, a square white plate had been nailed to the wall. *Nonsmoking room.* Nick's vantage was from the bed, apparently where Emma was in the vision. Her attention moved to the door and stayed there, and Nick knew she heard or sensed someone coming. Sure enough, the doorknob turned, and the woman from the parking-lot fight entered. Nick saw her clearly now. Her hair wasn't blond; it was pale gray. Her eyes weren't black or gray, but somewhere in between. Charcoal. Her left eye was swollen shut. As she edged forward, Nick saw that her entire face looked as though she'd been hit with a baseball bat, but he knew better; he'd seen the man and the way he'd wielded his fist like a prizefighter.

Her eyes darted nervously from Emma to the door and back again. Then she held out a hand and said something to Emma. Nick couldn't make out her words, because her mouth was too swollen to read her lips. But he knew Emma's answer. She shook her head, obviously not wanting to leave with the woman.

The woman's right eye narrowed until it was almost as closed as the left one, and she grabbed Emma's hand and said something else, her busted lip moving rapidly with the words. Whatever she said worked, because Emma nodded and then followed her outside.

"Hey, baby." The low purr was beside his left ear, and the owner of the voice was so close that Nick felt the heat of her words against his skin, not to mention the smell of tequila on her breath.

Shit. He lost the connection because of a hooker.

"Do you have any more?" she continued.

"Any more?" Nick questioned.

"Of whatever got you so trashed that you didn't see me flashing you my goods." She smiled, displaying a prominent gap between her front two teeth, then she leaned toward him, pushed her shoulders forward and offered him a closer look at the cleavage already on display. Her right tit was pierced. "I'll do you for half," she crooned.

Nick shook his head. "Thanks, but I've gotta go."
He turned, got back in the hotter-than-hell Taurus
and drove away. He'd seen more during his connection with Emma than he ever had before, but he still
had nothing he could work with. Even seeing the
woman's face wasn't going to help. She'd been
beaten so badly that her features weren't anywhere
near normal, and she had no unique identifying
traits. He had no idea what she looked like when she
wasn't swollen, black and blue.

His cell phone rang as he drove up the ramp
leading to I-10 and New Orleans. He unclipped the
phone from his belt and jabbed the speaker button,
then increased his speed on the interstate. "Madere."

"Nick, you learned anything? Tell me you've got
something we can work with." Jeff Stewart wasn't
known for his telephone manners, at least not when
it came to his coworkers. Thank goodness he was a
little better dealing with the victims' families.

"Nothing concrete, but I'm getting there. I went
to the hotel where they were staying."

"And?"

"Nothing concrete," Nick repeated, holding back
the description he had of the woman, since he really
couldn't describe her worth a damn due to her
beating. "But I'll get something soon. Things are
falling into place."

"Well, they better fall quickly. You've got two
days."

"Two days?" Nick wove through increasing traffic as he moved closer to the city. It was getting darker. He looked ahead to see the Superdome, its giant bowl shape producing a prominent shadow to the left of the interstate. He was nearly to his house. "Why two days?" He wanted to find Emma quickly too, but he wasn't aware of a deadline.

"Ronald Moore said he's taking the new lead to the media Monday morning. He's giving us the weekend, and then he's going to let every news station around know that she was sighted in Louisiana."

"Could you not—" Nick didn't get a chance to finish asking why Jeff couldn't talk sense into the man. Stewart obviously knew Nick well enough to know where the question was heading.

"He's lost his daughter, Nick. I don't blame him for wanting to do everything in his power to bring her back, but you and I both know that the chances of bringing her back alive, if indeed she's in Louisiana, are better if we don't let the kidnappers know we're onto them. I tried my damnedest to explain that, and I was able to get him to agree to wait until Monday. If I were you, I'd be glad you got that, and make the most of the next two days. No, scratch that. *Find* her in the next two days. You understand?" Jeff ordered.

"Perfectly." Nick disconnected and turned onto Orange Street. Within seconds, he pulled into the familiar cobbled driveway and stared at his home.

There weren't many New Orleans homes that hadn't been harmed by Katrina, but his was one of the lucky ones. It wasn't nearly as large as the ones around it; nonetheless, it stood out, thanks to years of Nick putting every spare dime and hours of elbow grease into its restoration. He'd bought it for practically nothing, due to its dilapidated state, and hadn't begrudged one moment of the work it took to make it shine again. He'd planned to live here forever, get married and raise kids here, and be close to his family.

Nick took a moment to examine his handiwork. Outdoor lighting, all in an elaborate black metal, spotlighted the place as though it were the White House. Nick hadn't wanted the house to look empty, so he'd set the lights on a timer. He was glad he had; the home deserved to be spotlighted. Ornate cast ironwork decorated the porches that stretched across the front of the house, one on the top story, one on the bottom, and the lighting hit the swirling designs to cast black lace shadows over the white siding. A small garden graced one side of the house, and Nick was thankful he'd paid a landscape company to keep it up while he was gone. Centered on the tiny green lawn, a bright blue birdbath reflected the streetlight. This was a home to be proud of, and Nick suddenly wished there was some way to show it to his fantasy woman.

Thinking of her, he returned to Emma Moore's

file. The hooker had cut off the visions just as Emma's mind had started to open to him. Somehow, she was connected to his dream girl, and maybe if Nick figured out how, he'd find Emma *and* the brunette beauty.

A swirl of black and gray claimed his sight, and then Nick was back in the car and staring at the woman driving, who continued to glance toward the backseat and appeared to be reassuring her passengers. What had happened to the man, and what role did this new woman play in Emma's kidnapping? Nick struggled to hold on to this vision; he needed to know where they were going. He actually felt a pull, but he fought it. How long could he keep the next image at bay? The car was slowing, the trees outside the window appearing more clearly as Nick focused on the surroundings settling into place. A little more...

The car turned onto a dirt road, and Nick peered through the front window. They drove slowly, brown dust kicking up as they progressed, and then Nick saw it. The brick building that he'd seen before. It was longer than he'd previously realized, like a house that had been added onto a few times. He saw the thick hedge filled with clusters of pink roses completely covering one side, but that was the only identifying feature. Obviously, this wasn't a home, but if it was a business, there was no indication. There was no signage at all, nothing to let Nick know the location or the name of the place.

The car slowed to a stop, more dust shielding the brick building from view as it did. Then the air cleared, and one of the doors to the building opened.

Again, Nick felt the pull of the vision trying to change, and again, he concentrated hard to hold on a little longer. He had to see who exited that building.

An elderly black woman stepped outside. She wore an old-fashioned blue seersucker dress with a white apron tied around her waist. Her head tilted to the side as she peered toward the car, and then she smiled easily and clapped her hands together as though eager to meet her guests. The woman in the front seat climbed out, said something to the elderly woman, and then opened the backdoor to allow her passengers to exit.

Emma remained on her side of the vehicle, but she turned and watched the woman next to her gingerly climb out, her body obviously still sore from her beating. The woman reached toward Emma. Her face was bruised even more than it had been when Nick saw her at the hotel, with that day-after effect that made a victim look worse instead of better.

Emma looked toward the building, then toward the elderly woman and the woman who'd been driving, and then back to the battered lady reaching for her hand. She didn't move.

The woman leaned farther into the car and said something, and then Emma eased across the seat and climbed out. Again, she took in her surroundings, and Nick took advantage of her curiosity to search for more clues to her location. The land was barren, with sparse patches of grass sprinkling the area around the home. The only dominant landscaping was the rose hedge along one side, though Nick could see that tiny shrubs had been planted down the length of the place.

The brown-haired woman who'd been driving looked at Emma and said something. Nick watched her lips carefully, and made out, "We're glad you're here."

Glad she was there? What did that mean? What kind of sick people had taken the girl, and what were they planning to do with her? This didn't *feel* right.

Emma looked from the driver to the elderly woman, who was also speaking. Then all of their attention turned back to the building. A striking woman exited, and like the others, she smiled broadly. She wore a bright blue shirt that mirrored the dramatic blue of her eyes, and long blond waves tumbled well past her shoulders. She spoke to Emma, but Nick didn't catch the words, because she turned as she was speaking to look back toward the door. As Nick and Emma watched, another woman exited.

His mouth went dry. What the hell was she doing here?

Nick blinked, and found himself thrust out of the connection completely and back sitting in the rental in his driveway. The air blasting his face from the car vents reminded him he hadn't turned off the ignition. Yet even with the air on high, he was sweating, not from the New Orleans heat this time, but from the shock, the intensity, of what he'd seen. The kidnappers had taken Emma to some sort of…convent? And his sexy brunette had been there.

He'd wondered why he always ended up with her whenever he connected with Emma; now he knew. They were in the same damn place. Had that bedroom where they'd had countless bouts of marathon sex been right down the hall from her? And was Emma being harmed in any way in that big brick building? The bunch of women hadn't appeared to have been doing anything sinister in the vision, but hell, what were they doing taking her there, and away from her parents? Were they a cult? Some type of baby-selling ring? And how was his fantasy woman involved?

God help her if she was part of the kidnapping.

Baffled by this new information, he climbed from the car, gathered his things and started toward the house.

God help him, too—he was back home.

10

DELORES HAD PAID careful attention to everything
she'd been told about the shelter, from when she
first called the hotline and asked for help, to the
detailed conversation she'd had with Rosa yesterday. Everything they'd told her had assured her that
Marcus wouldn't find her, that she and Hannah
would be safe within the confines of the brick buildings composing the Seven Sisters.

   The location of the shelter was guarded relig-
iously, and the place didn't have any identification
that would lead anyone to believe it was a haven for
battered women and abused children. Furthermore,
you could barely even see the buildings from the
street, thanks to the long, winding dirt path that set
it off of East Saint Bernard Highway. And another
advantage was that the shelter was in Chalmette, an
area still grossly in need of rebuilding after Katrina.
Most of the businesses that had once dominated the
city were still boarded up, with no plans to reopen
until their funding came in from their insurance
companies or the state. Some places looked as

though they'd never reopen, having been flooded completely and left to rot in the heat of the Louisiana sun. During the drive with Kayla, Delores had even noticed a car dealership whose cars had been left abandoned, tossed about and mud-ridden, after Katrina. No doubt, if she didn't want Marcus to find her, he wouldn't.

But she didn't *want* to hide from Marcus. They had been together since she was a teen and he was in his twenties, the big truck driver that'd stolen her heart and driven her into the sunset, leaving her father—and her father's fists—behind. Marcus had always protected her, had always loved her, really loved her. How many times had he told her that no other man would love her like he did? And how many times had he calmed her during her nightmares, when she'd remember so vividly the way her father had been?

Her father beat her just because he could. Marcus would never do that. He'd hit her, sure, but only when she deserved it. And it wasn't all that often. This time had been worse than any other, because she'd questioned his authority about the girl. She shouldn't have done that. She should've listened to him. It had seemed wrong to make her do something she didn't want to do, but Marcus had reminded Delores how good he treated all of their girls. They got new clothes regular-like, and always had something to eat. And they wanted to do what they did.

She frowned. That was what had bothered her about Hannah. She didn't choose to come with them like the others had. She wasn't leaving a rough family life. In fact, she'd had it very good, from what Delores could tell.

Delores shook away that thought. She'd made her mind up that going back to Marcus would be best. She just had to make sure that he'd calmed down and would forgive her for running away and taking Hannah. Maybe she could convince him to let Hannah wait a while, until she was older, before she went out with the other girls.

She touched her cheek. It wasn't nearly as sore now, and her eye had opened completely, the cut below it nearly healed. It might not even scar much, thanks to the salve Rosa had provided.

Marcus probably felt terrible about hitting her so hard. He always felt bad about it, and usually made it up to her by taking her on a shopping trip. He'd buy her some pretty things, then they'd eat out and go back to the hotel and…

Hannah moaned in her sleep. Delores glanced at the girl, moved toward her and placed a hand to her cheek. She wasn't warm, so she probably didn't have a fever or anything, even if she hadn't been acting so good. But that was probably just her way of pouting about not talking. Delores had used the same threat Marcus had used to keep Hannah from causing trouble after he'd taken her. He'd told her to stay quiet in public, or he'd go back and get her little sister too. Delores had simply followed his lead after she took Hannah from him by telling the little girl that her sister would be okay as long as she didn't tell anyone who she really was, or how she came to be with Delores.

The lie had worked. Hannah hadn't said anything about Delores or Marcus to the women at the shelter. She hadn't said anything at all. Delores hadn't meant to scare her that much and had finally taken her aside this morning and tried to explain in kid terms that she could speak, just not about what had happened. Hannah had nodded like she understood, and Delores guessed that she had, since Rosa mentioned that Hannah had spoken to Jenee.

At first, Delores had felt a surge of panic when she'd heard that Hannah had actually talked to the Vicknair girl. But she hadn't told Jenee anything she shouldn't; if she had, the police would have shown by now. Apparently, Hannah had simply needed to talk. Which was all fine and dandy as long as she didn't say too much.

Delores was no dummy. Eventually, Hannah would say more. She was just a little girl, after all, and little girls tended to trust adults. So before that could happen, the two of them would need to get far, far away from the shelter.

Hannah whimpered in her sleep, and Delores frowned. She hated it that she was so sad. She seemed sadder now than when they'd been in that hotel with Marcus and the other girls. Maybe going back to Marcus would help her feel better. After she got used to everything, she'd maybe even like it like the other ones did. And surely she'd like getting some new clothes. The shelter provided clothing for both of them, but it wasn't the kind of clothes that Marcus bought. He liked to get the shiny stuff, with sequins or glitter, especially for the girls. Guys liked the shiny stuff.

And they liked the girls.

Delores looked at the tiny person in the bed. Her mind was fighting itself over what to do, and she knew it. Having Hannah do what the others did was wrong. But not going back to Marcus…wasn't an option. Delores needed him. She simply wasn't right without him. And if she came back without Hannah, he wouldn't stop with a beating. And she'd deserve whatever she got. She had disobeyed him, after all.

She simply couldn't go back without Hannah.

And she had to go back.

Taking another peek to make sure Hannah was good and asleep, Delores crept from their room and moved silently down the hall. She heard the two teens, Ellie and Chylia, chatting with a couple of the volunteers, women who'd come to the shelter this morning before Jenee had left for the day. Jenee seemed very interested in Hannah and Delores, too interested, so Delores thought it'd be better to contact Marcus while she was gone.

Unfortunately, Rosa and Kayla had both told her that the shelter had no telephones to communicate with the outside world. The reason was to keep abusive husbands and parents from trying to contact the shelter and locate their wives and children. Instead of a regular phone, they used cell phones, and those numbers changed regularly. But Delores had seen one of the volunteers use her cell phone earlier, and she'd also watched the woman when she tucked it in one of the storage cubbies near the door.

Delores cautiously looked around as her hand slid into the cubby and withdrew the cell phone. Then, she moved to the nearest room, the reading room, which was blessedly empty, and dialed Marcus.

JENEE'S SHOULDERS ACHED, the back of her neck burned and her fingertips were nearly raw—typical responses to a Saturday workday at the Vicknair plantation. They'd been hard at it since eight that morning, and she was extremely thankful that the sun was in the process of dropping, since that was Nanette's signal that they could call it a full day. Jenee really didn't mind the weekly ritual, getting together with the family to help keep the home standing. They'd started the routine shortly after Katrina, when Charles Roussel, the parish president, had deemed the place a hazard and placed it on the top of his demolition list. Luckily, the historical society was considering funding the necessary repairs to the plantation, but that would only be decided after renovations on the homes in Jefferson parish, where more of the tourists visited, were completed first.

So until then, every Saturday found all of the family members on hand doing the repairs themselves, though occasionally, Gage would have to pull duty at the hospital or Tristan would be on call at the firehouse. Today, however, everyone was here, and it was a good thing, with the next inspection by the historical society scheduled for the following week. Thanks to Nanette's research, the family knew the best way to obtain money from the society was to show that they were already making progress toward the goal. And they were. The house was in much better shape than it'd been a year ago, and even with its problems, it was inhabitable—something that couldn't have been said right after Katrina hit land.

As usual, Nanette had a plan for the day and had put everyone working on something the moment they'd arrived. Today's goals had consisted of putting up drywall on the first floor and replacing the worst portions of the stairs. The male Vicknairs had wasted no time taking charge of replacing the drywall, while Jenee, Chantelle and Celeste took on the stairs, sanding the rough spots on the salvageable ones and prying up the others and replacing them with something decent enough to stand the weight of a human. Eventually, all of the stairs would need to be replaced, but for now, they simply wanted the things to be safe.

The pregnant females, Monique and Kayla, busied themselves in the kitchen cooking lunch and dinner for the mass of Vicknairs, and Nanette had busied herself fighting—and flirting, in Jenee's opinion—with Charles Roussel. The parish president had been by the house no less than three times throughout the day, primarily to shake his head and let them know they were wasting their time. The society had "just about decided that this place wasn't worth the ground it stood on," according to Roussel, and then he'd asked Nanette if she wanted to go out to dinner tonight to discuss the family's options. Even though Nanette had told him he must be three crawfish short of a pound to think she'd go out with him, Jenee hadn't missed the slight pause before her response, or the sudden loss of her typical guarded composure. She'd looked completely shocked by his offer, but she'd also looked secretly *pleased.*

Jenee had been around Nanette her entire life, and she wasn't fool enough to miss the fact that there was more—much more—to Nan and Charles Roussel's feud than any of the cousins knew.

If it were any of the other cousins, Jenee would

simply ask what was up between the two of them and would probably get an answer. But Nanette had always been much more independent, more private, than the rest. Maybe it was because she was the oldest, or maybe it was because she was the only cousin without siblings. But either way, Jenee knew asking her about what was really going on between her and Charles would only piss her off, and no one wanted Nanette pissed, particularly on a Vicknair workday, when she controlled their schedule.

When Charles came by after their late lunch, Nanette had practically shoved him into his black Mercedes and told him not to come back, but it really hadn't surprised Jenee when he returned a couple of hours later.

"What is it about those two?" Chantelle asked, plopping down beside Jenee on the bottom step in the plantation's foyer. They'd chatted throughout their work on the stairs, primarily about the shelter and Jenee's progress with Hannah, but right now, their conversation focused on the two people feuding and flirting outside. The front door was open, as it'd been all day, to allow what little breeze there was from the Mississippi to find its way into the house, and to attempt to clear some of the drywall dust that the guys had generated in the bottom rooms. It now also conveniently served as an easy method for viewing the heated conversation currently taking place between Nanette and the parish president.

Jenee sipped on her reward for finishing the stairs, a big glass of iced sweet tea, and then shook her head. "I don't know, but if you ask me, Nanette and Charles Roussel have been dancing around that line for a good ten years."

"What line is that?" Celeste asked, sitting behind them and rubbing her palms back and forth against the sides of her own chilled glass of tea.

"The thin line between love and hate," Jenee answered as Nanette, her face flushed and her long black hair swinging slightly as her head moved with every word, stepped toward the sexy Cajun currently serving as head of the parish and consequently, head of the historical society.

"Bet you anything he's smiling right now," Celeste said. They couldn't tell, since his back faced them. All they could see was Nanette's face, obviously angry, her green eyes flashing. "She hates it when he smiles. Says he has a devil's dimple, whatever that means."

"That's a dimple in one cheek, and it's called a devil's dimple because supposedly a guy who has one has complete control over women, whether they want him to have it or not," Jenee explained. "And Nanette probably can't stand the way that dimple affects her."

"She does like to be in control, and he does seem to be the only guy around who can make her lose it," Celeste agreed.

"Well, he does have a killer smile." Chantelle lifted her tea glass toward the door as she spoke, presumably saluting the main object of the conversation. "You've got to admit, it's hard to pass one of his campaign posters on River Road without doing a double take."

Jenee knew Celeste and Chantelle were probably picturing Roussel's posters, where he smiled as though he'd won the lottery…no, that wasn't it. In those pictures, Charles Roussel looked as if he'd just had amazing sex. And that realization led her thoughts to another smile, the smile on her ghost's face when he was *about to have* amazing sex. Merely thinking of that smile, those turquoise eyes, made her wet. She'd wondered if she'd see him today, since she was at the plantation where spirits often visited. She'd assumed it might even be easier to *feel* him here.

But she hadn't even sensed him, no matter how hard she'd tried, or how much she'd wanted to. It made her wonder if she *couldn't* bond with him here, if perhaps she could only be with him that way when she was at the shelter, which strengthened her theory that Hannah had something to do with her fantasy ghost's visits. Jenee frowned. He *wasn't* a ghost, even if she didn't know exactly what he was. Ghosts definitely never left anything behind, but her dream man had.

Her hand inadvertently moved toward the

pocket of her shorts and slipped inside, feeling the
proof that he'd really been there, those two
buttons she'd found on the floor of her bedroom
this morning.

"No way!"

Chantelle's exclamation snapped Jenee out of her
reverie, and she followed her sister-in-law's gaze to
the couple that had been arguing outside. But Nanette
and Charles weren't arguing now. In fact, they'd
swapped positions, and Nanette was backed against
his car, with Charles Roussel's hands clasping hers
and pressing them against the driver's window as he
pressed against her, kissing her as though he had no
intention of stopping—ever. Nanette squirmed beneath
him, and it wasn't totally clear whether she was trying
to get away…or get closer.

Jenee's gasp barely escaped her mouth before
Nanette finally wriggled from his embrace, took an off
balance step away, shook her head as though clearing
it and then reared back and slapped him. Hard.

"I was right," he said, while the three eavesdrop-
pers on the stairs leaned forward to hear.

Flustered, Nanette panted, "Right?"

"You still want me, Nanette Vicknair, even
though you don't *want* to want me—and you know
I still want you, even more than back then."

Nanette's mouth opened, but no words came out.

"Say yes, Nan. Go to dinner with me tonight.
Let's talk about what went wrong back then. I have

something I need to tell you, and I'm tired of playing this cat-and-mouse game. I messed up, and I want to get it right." His smile crooked up, and Jenee saw that devil's dimple dip in. "I know you want to, too."

Nanette took a deep breath, seemingly to gain her usual composure, then said softly, almost too low for Jenee to hear, "Obviously you don't know me as well as you think, Charles. Because if you did, you'd know that I never make the same mistake twice." Then she stormed toward the plantation where Jenee, Chantelle and Celeste sat, watching with dropped jaws. And Roussel, rubbing his cheek where she'd hit him, smiled like the dashing devil he was.

Nan glared at them with don't-say-a-word green eyes, and all of them were smart enough to heed the silent warning. Then she continued her trek toward the kitchen.

"What was that about—" Chantelle's words lodged in her throat as Nanette suddenly reappeared, moved to the doorway and stopped there, her legs braced apart like a cop ready to shoot. Good thing she didn't own a gun.

"Get off my property, Roussel. Now."

Jenee leaned to the side so she could get a better view of the man still standing by the car, his head cocked as though questioning whether Nanette meant what she said. Then his smile broadened and he winked at her. "You don't mean that, *chère*. Let's finish our talk." Even Jenee could see his gaze drop from Nanette's eyes to her lips.

"I'll call the police," she added, her voice low and threatening. "Or better yet…" She pivoted toward the room that had at one time served as a formal dining area, but was currently filled with Vicknair men and a bunch of drywall materials. "Tristan," she called, again in a calm tone that totally betrayed the anger bristling just beneath the surface. Jenee could see it, and undoubtedly so could Roussel, though it didn't seem to be bothering the guy. In fact, he looked as though he was totally enjoying the situation.

Jenee wasn't about to mention that to Nanette. Or anyone else within earshot of Nan.

When all of the hammering and banging and cussing continued on the other side of the plastic separating the dining room from the foyer, Nanette yelled, "Tris-tan!"

Within seconds, the hammering subsided and Tristan, his clothing smudged with drywall mud, stepped out from behind the paint-splattered sheet. "Hell, Nanette. What is it?"

"You still got your .22 upstairs? If you do, I need it. I've got a rodent to kill."

Charles Roussel's laughter echoed from outside. "That won't be necessary, Vicknair. It just so happens, I was ready to leave anyway."

"Fancy that," Nan said, then crossed her arms at her chest and leaned against one side of the doorway until he was safely in his Mercedes and heading down their driveway, a gray cloud of dust billowing in his wake. "And good riddance."

"Nanette," Jenee started.

"Not talking about it. Not now, not ever," she stated, and stomped toward the back of the house for the second time, the swinging door in the hall flapping loudly behind her as she entered the kitchen.

"What happened?" Tristan looked from Roussel's retreating Mercedes to the kitchen door, still bouncing on its hinges down the hall.

"Roussel was kissing her outside," Chantelle told her husband. "And it was no peck on the cheek, either."

Tristan nodded as though the news was no surprise whatsoever. "Yeah, I kind of wondered how long they'd sit on it."

"Sit on what?" Jenee asked.

"That attraction between them. Figured they'd either kill each other or finally let the tension take over." He winked at Chantelle. "Sometimes it's fun to fuss with the one you want."

"Hey, I can't help it that you were stubborn," she said, not missing a beat.

"*I* was stubborn?"

She shrugged, and Tristan laughed, then disappeared behind the plastic sheeting.

"So, if Nanette happened to hook up with Roussel for something long term, that'd leave only one Vicknair in the *available* category," Chantelle mused, focusing her pale blue eyes on Jenee.

Jenee felt blood tinge her cheeks, and she couldn't hide her response. Chantelle, ever observant, was on her in a flash.

"What do you think, Celeste? Does that look like someone with a secret to you?"

Celeste leaned forward, peeked at Jenee's face and nodded. "Definitely."

"Care to tell us his name?" Chantelle's blond brows lifted with curiosity.

Jenee laughed. His name. She couldn't even tell *herself* his name. She twisted to sit sideways on the step, so she could look at both of them as she spoke. Then she sipped her tea, figuring a bit of caffeine wouldn't hurt when having this conversation, and said, "I'd tell you his name, if I knew it."

"You don't know his name?" Celeste's voice suddenly took on a serious tone. "Jenee, are we talking about someone you've slept with?"

Jenee's free hand drifted back to her pocket, and she slid it inside. She supposed that throughout the day, she'd half expected the buttons that'd fallen from his shirt when she'd been so eager to have him naked to disappear, but they hadn't. They were still there, and her reaction to feeling them was the same as it'd been every other time she'd felt them throughout the day. Sheer exhilaration. It *had* been real.

"You've slept with the guy, and you don't even

know his name?" Unfortunately, Chantelle's question was delivered at a moment when there was a lull in the hammering in the next room. In less than a second, the plastic sheet whipped back again to reveal Tristan's head, covered in so much drywall dust now that he looked prematurely gray. But Jenee wasn't about to mention that, or anything else remotely funny right now, not while her brother was so intensely focused on her—and silently awaiting her response.

When she didn't speak, he did.

"Since the other two women in the foyer are married, one of them to me, I'm assuming that remark was geared toward you," he said, sounding more like a father than a big brother.

"It's not what you think, Tristan," Jenee said, and hated it that she suddenly felt the way she had at fourteen, when Tristan had cornered her after her first kiss. Was it her fault that one of his friends had given her a lesson in the art of tonsil hockey behind the Vicknair shed? Or that her big brother picked that precise moment to exit the cane field and see Jenee doing her best to learn everything Rob was willing to teach? Of course, the fact that she was learning to kiss wasn't the problem; the fact that she was fourteen and Tristan's buddy was nineteen… that had been the stumbling block. And the thing that had caused Tristan's fist to collide with Rob's head.

"You're sleeping with a guy and you don't know his name," Tristan repeated, his voice deceivingly calm. "Is that right?"

She nodded. "But…"

"And you say it's not what I think. You tell me how it isn't what I think."

"He's—different." She couldn't say it without smiling, which predictably didn't go over so well with her brother. She was suddenly glad her handsome ghost wasn't around, just in case Tristan's fist was able to traverse the boundary between the living and the whatever-he-was. It'd be a shame to mess up that gorgeous face, or to see her ghost take a whirl at Tristan's, because as formidable a force as Tristan was with his traditional firefighter build— long, lean and muscled—she wasn't sure how he'd fare against her ghost, who looked as though he could handle anything…and anyone. He sure knew how to handle Jenee. Tristan's eyes narrowed even further as Jenee couldn't keep her smile contained.

Gage, Dax and Ryan all suddenly emerged from behind the sheet to join Tristan in scrutinizing Jenee. This wasn't exactly the way she'd planned to tell them about her dream guy.

"Exactly how different is he? And why would his being different keep you from knowing his name?" Tristan asked, then muttered a word Jenee hadn't heard him say in quite a while, at least not since he'd married Chantelle.

"Tristan," Chantelle chided.

"Jenee, what have you been doing?" he demanded, too focused on his sister to respond to his wife.

Okay. Since their folks had moved to Florida when Jenee was merely a sophomore at LSU, Tristan had watched after her a little more diligently than a typical big brother would. She hadn't minded, until now, but she was twenty-two, dammit. She had no need for his overzealous monitoring of what she did or who she saw, or who she slept with, for that matter.

Apparently, Tristan knew her well enough to see that she'd gone from the defensive to the offensive, and thought his drywall-dusted head looked like a good target. His eyes widened at her glare, and he had the nerve to laugh.

"Fine. Fine." He held up his palms as though Jenee would actually hit him. Not a bad move, since she *was* giving it careful consideration.

"Fine, what?" she asked.

"Fine, I'm sure there's a good reason for what— what Chantelle said. So tell me what it is, sis, if you don't mind."

The kitchen door opened, and Nanette, Monique and Kayla appeared in the hall. Obviously, the house was quiet enough now that everyone had heard at least a portion of this unconventional conversation and wanted to get in on the latest gossip. Funny how the attention had so quickly moved from

Nanette and Charles Roussel to Jenee and her unnamed dream man.

"What's going on?" Monique asked.

Ryan put his arm around his wife and answered her question. "Jenee's about to tell us about the guy she's been sleeping with." He grinned. "Hey, this is turning out to be the most interesting Vicknair workday since I joined the family. First Nanette and Roussel are all but having sex against his Mercedes—"

"We were not," Nanette snapped.

"Hey, the windows in that front room are dusty, but I saw what I saw," Ryan answered with a shrug. "And now Jenee admits she's sleeping with a guy and doesn't know his name." He grinned, obviously knowing he was pushing all kinds of hot buttons and enjoying it.

Nanette held up a warning finger, as though daring anyone to agree with Ryan's point regarding what had happened between her and Roussel. And then she looked at Ryan as though he'd better be extra careful when he ate anything from her kitchen.

Ryan grinned again, and Jenee couldn't hold back a smile. Yeah, he was having a little fun at her expense, but ever since Ryan had come back to the land of the living, he'd truly enjoyed poking fun at life in general. It just so happened today was her day to be in his hot seat.

Ever since he'd come back to the land of the living.

Jenee surveyed him intently.

"Jenee?" Monique questioned.

"Ryan, how did you do it?" Jenee asked. "How did you stay on this side?"

"Oh, my word," Nanette mumbled, one hand moving in front of her mouth as she shook her head in disbelief. "You're sleeping with a ghost."

11

SOMETHING HAD CHANGED. Nick had been trying to connect with Emma all day and had come up empty every damn time. Not completely empty, but close enough. He'd see the same visions he'd seen before, the ride through the swamp, the long brick building, the fight at the hotel, the book-filled room—all of the images he'd previously seen and nothing more. That alone bothered him, but what made things worse was that in the image of the book-filled room, he always lost contact before the brunette arrived. Ditto for the image of the car arriving at the building. In fact, not one of his visions today had taken him where he'd so desperately wanted to go…

Back to her.

Because he knew one thing for certain— wherever Emma Moore had been taken, the brunette was there too.

Where the hell were they?

As a last resort, he'd driven back to the hotel and parked not far from the spot where he'd been yesterday. The sun had dipped down completely when he rolled down the windows and cut the engine. Thank God there was a slight breeze, or he'd have to get out of the vehicle, and he wanted to simply survey the place for a while before the scantily clad piranhas closed in.

The blonde who'd propositioned him yesterday leaned against the brick wall outside of a room, one leg bent to rest the heel of her thigh-high boot on the window ledge behind her. She wore hot-pink panties, clearly visible from her stance, and Nick was just grateful she wore any at all. Otherwise— well, he didn't want to think of the view he'd have right now if she hadn't. Her tube top stretched so tight across her ample chest that Nick could see the outline of her nipple ring beneath the fabric.

She tilted her head and surveyed Nick's car, but thankfully, the Taurus had tinted windows, yet another method of combating the New Orleans heat, and from the angle he was parked, she could only view the front of the car—no chance at seeing Nick through the open side windows. She took a step in his direction, but then a man called out to her from the corner of the building, and she sashayed his way.

Nick scanned the women surrounding the building. The setup was perfect for the operation they were running. The hotel had one side facing Veterans Boulevard, but that side was void of this type of action. As a matter of fact, as Nick had driven up, he'd wondered if anyone was staying in the hotel at all, because there'd seemed to be no activity. All the curtains were drawn, and there was no sign of life…from that side of the street. Back here, however, was a different story.

It was an effective way of handling business. With everyone on this side, away from easy street access, their work environment was virtually hidden from drivers, and from cops. Nick assumed that the guy in charge, presumably the man that had called pierced nipple to the corner, had someone on the other side looking out for patrol cars. If one was spotted, all of the girls perched so conveniently outside of their rented rooms could simply walk inside and close the doors until the threat disappeared. Not a bad setup indeed.

Nick made a mental note to mention this to Maurice LeBraud when he saw him. Nick's old boss still often worked with the NOPD, and this operation would be right up his alley. Nick could blow the whistle himself, but he didn't exactly want it blown quite yet. This hotel had something to do with Emma's disappearance, and until he found out what, he'd let the women of the night have their run of the place.

He reached for Emma's file, as he'd done several times throughout the day, and opened it. He had one more day to find her, or her father would blow the lid right off this case, and send the kidnappers running. Nick couldn't stand the thought of that, because it meant possibly losing Emma…and the woman in his dreams.

Dreams. Not exactly the way to look at it, given that somehow he'd left those buttons behind.

He shook his head. There wasn't any time to analyze that now. He really needed to find Emma again. Opening the manila folder, he was drawn to those eyes. They were big, almond shaped, and so dark that he couldn't tell where the iris ended and the pupil began. "Come on, *chère*. Take me further this time. Show me how this hotel factors into everything."

As if by command, the image of the parking lot filled his mind, but in the vision, it was much darker outside than it was now. The man's fist sailed through the air and collided with the woman's cheek, and Emma's tears blurred everything in sight. Nick focused…focused…strained to see more. Some kind of clue. There had to be something he'd missed, something he didn't see…

Emma's attention flew from the man and woman to the two teens, sparsely dressed and intent on pulling her away from the fight and back to their room.

Their room. Nick's eyes flew open, the vision halted by the sudden jolt of realization. "Hell."

He exited the car.

His "friend" from yesterday spotted him immediately and staked her claim, her boots clomping loudly as she worked it across the parking lot, glaring at the other women. "Mine," she said, slowing her pace and throwing a more provocative swing into her hips. Tonight's ensemble was the red tube top he'd noticed earlier, black leather mini-skirt, thigh-high boots—and hot-pink panties, he knew from her earlier stance. This outfit exposed the fact that her belly button was also pierced, and circled by a tattooed wreath of roses.

"I knew you'd come back," she purred. "Tall, dark, big and sexy. I remember you." She winked, an abundance of fake lashes tapping her cheek with the action.

Nick nodded.

"My offer still stands," she said huskily. "I'll do you for half…the first time."

"I just need to ask you a couple of questions," Nick said, wanting to head her off before she literally crawled on top of him in the parking lot. She didn't look above doing it, right here, right now.

That fan of fake lashes splayed across her brows, her eyes grew so wide. "You gotta be shittin' me. You want to *talk?*" Then her head shook slightly and all of her hair shifted. A wig, no big surprise. "Hell, you're some sort of cop, aren't you?" She started to look back toward the building, where her pimp would undoubtedly notice her skittish behavior.

Nick quickly moved his hand behind her neck and held it in place, firmly keeping her attention on him and hoping like hell that it appeared he was eager for her to give him what she was offering.

"Listen," he said, his voice low and steady. "I'm not here to take you in. I just need answers to some questions, and I don't need your man over there interfering, or this could get ugly. Understand?"

Eyes still wide, she nodded.

"Can I talk to you—*just* talk to you—for a few minutes?"

Dark brows furrowed, and she pursed her lips. "Twenty bucks."

"What?"

"I can't very well stand out here and talk to you without Willie getting suspicious. We'll go in my room and talk, and you'll pay me twenty for it."

"I'm not—"

"Then I'm not either," she said with a shrug, surveying her red clawlike nails.

Nick scrubbed his hand down his face, pulled his wallet from his pocket and watched her eyes flare again.

"Are you crazy? No money out here." She turned, indicated the room behind where she'd been standing. "Follow me."

Nick did, and wondered how he'd explain *this* to Jeff Stewart if the place ended up getting raided while he was in the hooker's room.

She waited for him to enter then closed the door. "You seriously just want to talk?"

"Seriously," Nick said, taking a seat in a chair near the door, while she stretched out on the bed.

"Amazing how many guys just want to talk nowadays. Or watch. Whatever. Normally I make them pay full price, but since you're a cop and all…you are a cop, aren't you?"

"Something like that. I'm looking for a little girl…"

"Damn, you don't even look the type."

Nick checked his fury at that remark. "Not like that. Or, maybe, exactly like that," he added in retrospect. "The thing is I'm trying to find a little girl that was kidnapped two weeks ago in Atlanta. I have good reason to believe that she's been here at some point, staying with a man and woman, and two teen girls."

"How old?"

"Eleven, but she's small for her age." A flicker of hope stirred within him. Had she seen Emma?

"Not kidnapped, you mean. She's a runaway, right? Ran away from home?"

Nick could tell she knew something. "No, she was taken. Kidnapped, like I said." He'd seen Emma crying in that vision and knew better than to believe the little girl had left her parents and her home on her own accord. Not that it wasn't possible, but those visions just "felt" like she was taken. And he had a major tendency to trust his gut; it hadn't steered him wrong yet. "Have you seen a couple here with three girls? Two older teens and one younger?"

"The girls I saw were runaways. They were doing this, you know, 'cause they didn't want to go home. And the people with them, they were treating them good."

"The man and woman with them, you mean?" Nick asked, trying to determine whether she'd seen the same two that he'd seen in his vision. "It was a man and woman, wasn't it? Do you remember what they looked like, or their names?"

"No names, but I remember them good enough. Guy was balding. Woman was, I don't know, maybe late forties, early fifties. Normal-looking. They had two teens with them, one girl had a pink stripe in her hair, here." She took her finger from her left temple down past her cheek. "She was the skinnier one. The other was kinda chunky, but in the right places, you know. The men liked them, some more than me. You never know, some always like the young ones better," she said with a huff. "I say, whatever works. There's plenty of guys wanting it in N'awlins to go around."

"What about the third girl?" Nick asked, literally feeling the adrenaline surging within his veins. This was as close as he'd gotten, if she'd seen Emma. "Did you see her? How did she look? Did you talk to her? Hear them say her name?"

"No names," she repeated. "We don't use names round here." She unzipped her boots as she spoke and then tossed them on the floor. "They called the pink-striped girl Pinky. The other one was Sass. Not all that original, if you ask me, but they didn't. Ask me, I mean."

"What about the younger one?" Nick repeated, growing impatient.

"They didn't call her nothing, because she wasn't *doing* anything. She wasn't ready, I guess." She reached for the television remote and flipped on the channel. "*CSI*. My favorite. Damn, that Grissom is one sexy hunk of male. I'd sure let him play those whiskers around on me." She smiled toward the dusty television screen. "I'd do him for free."

Nick had been so engrossed in trying to draw out the woman that he'd forgotten that he'd brought the folder from the car. He grabbed it off the table beside him, moved toward the bed and opened it so that it blocked her view of the television. "Is that her? Is that the younger girl that you saw?" He tapped his finger beneath Emma's chin. "This one. Is she the girl that was with that couple and those teens?"

Grunting in annoyance, she nonetheless studied the picture. Then she shook her head. "Nope, that's not her."

Nick's stomach clenched. *That's not her.* "Are you sure?"

She sucked her top teeth with her tongue, then nodded. "Yep, I'm sure. Now let me watch the show a few more minutes before I have to get back to work." She looked past him, then cursed when a commercial claimed the screen.

Nick glanced at the photo before closing the file.

He'd been so sure that this woman knew something when she'd described the couple and the teens. He *knew* that they'd been at this hotel. The cybertip and his own vision verified it, but he'd wanted more. Something that would help him find Emma. If the couple had been staying here—and he knew they had—Nick felt fairly certain that their reason for doing so was to prostitute those teens. The girls had been dressed the part. Why hadn't he put it together earlier? Had his instincts been clouded by his lust for the brunette?

Whatever the cause, he had no doubt now. The reason they were at this particular hotel was because of its "special services."

He stood, then thought about the question he *hadn't* asked. "When did they leave? That couple, with the teens and the younger girl?"

She closed her eyes and appeared to think back, her red-glossed lips quirking to the side as she did. "I guess about a week ago. They were here a week, then left."

"Had you seen them before? The couple, I mean. Had they been here before?" Maybe it was the same couple, but at a different time, with different girls. They could still be the same ones in Nick's vision. The descriptions she'd provided would fit.

"A few times, but not all that often. They have to move around a lot, you know, when they're doing that."

Nick's skin bristled, the way it always did when he was nearing a lead. He pressed. "Doing what?"

"You know, with teens, doing the business with teens. It's risky enough for adults, but they're—" she shrugged "—they're teens. But hell, I was too when I started. And Willie saved me the same way."

Nick's skin was on fire now, he was so close to putting the pieces into place. "How? What do you mean that he saved you the same way? What way?"

"My family kicked me out. I was living on the streets, and Willie took me in, bought me clothes, gave me a place to live. All I had to do was…you know, whatever he needed me to do for the guys who like it young."

Nick knew about the teen-prostitute rings, particularly those that the feds had cracked down on recently that revolved around truck stops and rest areas predominantly in the southeastern section of the country. But he hadn't realized that these people were actually seen as something like a haven by the girls they took in.

He decided to try once more with Emma's photo, and put it back in front of her face. "Look again."

"You're making me miss my show," she snarled, but again, she looked. "And I'm telling you that's not the girl I saw."

"The picture is a year old. It was taken last summer, on a family trip to the beach. Maybe it doesn't look like her because she's a bit older."

Emma's parents had believed this photo depicted their child better than any other, had said it looked exactly like her. But what they weren't thinking at the time was that if Emma were being abused, she'd look nothing like the innocent, smiling face in this photograph. He'd chosen not to point that out to her parents, but now he wished that he had other photographs to work with. Some where she wasn't smiling, where she wasn't happy, because the girl whose eyes he'd peered through in this hotel's parking lot wasn't happy at all. She'd been crying her heart out. "Look again," Nick demanded.

"Listen here, Mr. Kinda-sorta Cop, that's not the girl I saw. The girl that was here didn't have no blond hair. Her hair was black as the Mississippi River after a hurricane. And shorter. Not nothing like the girl's hair in that picture, you hear?"

Nick swallowed, blinked, and looked at the photo—at the blond hair on Emma Moore. The woman with the cybertip had described the girl she saw at the hotel as blond, but who was to say that they hadn't tried to disguise Emma while they were here? That'd be the smart thing to do, and these kidnappers weren't dummies. Case in point, they hadn't been caught *yet.* "Look at her again," Nick said. "Could this be the same little girl, if her hair was black?"

"You think—what? That they dyed her hair or something? And chopped it off? Why would they do that? Guys usually like the little ones blond."

"Could have cut it. Could be a wig," Nick said, as though this wasn't nearly as big a deal as it was. "But either way, if her hair was black and shorter, could this be the same little girl?"

"I'm missing my show," she said, grumbling as she peered over the file to the television.

Nick grabbed the remote and punched the off button. "Could—it—be—her?"

"I'll take another look, if you give me another twenty." She fingered the top of her tube top, pulling it out a bit as she apparently checked the cash already stashed in her cleavage, then snapping the elastic back into place. "Yeah, twenty."

"You'll take another look, and really look at her, and *then* I'll give you another twenty." He held the folder up for her to view.

She grabbed it, pulling it away from Nick and toward the light beside the bed. Then she squinted, as though picturing the little girl with the hair he'd described.

"Well?" he prompted.

"Damn."

"What?" Nick asked, thinking he knew the answer.

"Shit, I think—yeah, with black hair, and if she was a little older, like you said—yeah, I think that's her. Humph, didn't think of that, but hell, we all change our hair, and things." She took another glance down at her boobs. "Got that twenty?"

"And you don't know where they went?" he

asked, tossing the bill on the bed and watching her long clawlike nails snatch it up and tuck it in her top.

"No."

Nick withdrew a card from his wallet and handed it to her. "If they do come back, especially in the next day, call that number. It's a hotline. Tell them you've seen Emma Moore, and they'll find me."

"Emma," she repeated. "Pretty name, too sweet for this business."

"She's not like those other girls. She didn't run away," Nick said, in case she hadn't clued in on that important fact. "She was taken from her parents, and she's probably scared to death."

"Hey, RoboCop," she jeered, still stretched out on the bed, and held up her hands in protest. "I didn't take her, and I won't be calling this number, at least not any time soon." She flicked the card onto the bedside table.

"Why's that?"

"Because they won't be back. The ones with the girls, the teens, the little ones, they're not like us. We can find our spot and stay there, as long as we don't make no trouble for the cops, you know. No offense," she added with a cheeky grin. "But the cops don't take kind to them bringing the young ones in, so those folks keep moving. Different hotels, truck spots, you know, moving all the time. They won't be back here for a while. Chances are they're done long gone from the bayou."

"They're still in the bayou," Nick said with conviction, before leaving the hooker looking skeptical in her hotel room.

Emma *was* still in Louisiana. He could feel it, sense it. She was in that brick building and with that woman from the hotel. Whether the man was still around wasn't certain; Nick hadn't seen the guy in any of the visions at the brick building. But the man and the woman were most definitely associated with a teen-prostitution ring. And they were also involved with Emma's kidnapping.

The woman in his fantasies was also involved in some way, though for the life of him, Nick couldn't figure out how. But he would. He had to find Emma, and he had to find *her*…and he had to do both by tomorrow.

No pressure.

12

BY THE TIME her brother had finished grilling her about how she'd ended up in bed with a nameless spirit, and the rest of the family had completed their attempt to determine why her particular apparition/ghost/whatever was so different than any other spirit they'd ever encountered, it was well past dark, Jenee was exhausted *and* she knew no more about her mystery man than she'd known before.

She took her time driving back to the shelter so she could think about everything they'd said. Merely a year ago, Ryan had been a ghost appearing to Monique, but unlike Jenee's dream man, a letter about him had arrived on Grandma Adeline's tea service for her cousin. He was dead and was supposed to have crossed over after he'd completed his assignment. But Ryan had fought the process, refusing to go because he wasn't ready to give up on life, or on Monique. And wonder of wonders, the powers that be had deemed him worthy of a second chance. Which was all fine and dandy for Ryan and Monique, but it didn't help Jenee at all. She hadn't received an assignment for her guy. No letter about him had shown up for her on the tea service, which wasn't surprising, given all her assigned spirits had been children. And he definitely wasn't.

Furthermore, Ryan and Monique said they were able to communicate when he was stuck in the middle. And from the looks on their faces when they mentioned that period of time, they'd done plenty of other things too. The same kinds of things Jenee had been doing with her spirit.

But Ryan and Monique had talked; they'd said so. And Ryan had been able to control when he came to Monique and when he left. Jenee knew her ghost couldn't control when he came to her or when he departed. She'd seen it in his eyes that last time, when he'd suddenly disappeared, and left her in midair.

She grinned, remembering how hard she had hit the floor. Did he even know that he'd literally left her hanging? Probably not. And she wondered if she'd ever get the chance to tell him. She hadn't sensed him at all today. What did that mean? Had he gone for good?

Her chest clenched, her throat tightened, and the threat of tears beckoned. Jenee couldn't bear the thought that she might never see him again. She wished she had some control…

Control. Dax and Celeste's situation had been different than Ryan's, because she'd had no control over when she saw Dax or how long she stayed. But Celeste had been hovering between life and death; somehow, Jenee didn't think that's what was going on with her spirit. Celeste had also said she could communicate with Dax when she saw him.

And there was another major difference between Jenee's ghost and Ryan and Celeste. His eyes. According to Monique, Ryan's eyes had been black, because he truly was a ghost in the middle. Celeste's had alternated between gray and black, since she was hovering between the two sides. Gray when she was closer to the land of the living, black when she was nearing the crossover stage.

But Jenee's ghost had the bluest eyes she'd ever seen, a brilliant turquoise as vivid as the Caribbean.

No one had an explanation for that. Or for the fact that he couldn't speak to Jenee.

She turned onto the dirt road leading to the shelter and racked her brain for some logical explanation. There had to be an answer, the same way there'd been an answer for Monique and Ryan's dilemma, and then Dax and Celeste's.

Jenee just had no idea what it was.

Parking her car behind the shelter, she got out and went inside to find Rosa seated in the kitchen, elbows on the table and her head bowed to rest within her weathered hands. She looked up when Jenee entered and the wrinkles on her face appeared even more prominent with her frown.

"What's wrong?" Jenee quickly crossed the room, her troubles with her fantasy man forgotten. "Did something happen? Is it Hannah?"

She didn't know why her mind immediately went to Hannah, maybe because she felt she'd made a breakthrough with the little girl last night when Hannah finally spoke, or maybe because she tugged at her heart. Or *maybe* it was the niggling guilt at having made a little progress toward getting Hannah to open up last night…and then being gone all day today. Should she have foregone the family work-day today for her?

"Rosa, is she okay?"

"She's okay, *chère,*" Rosa said, and apparently knowing the path Jenee's thoughts had taken, she added, "It wouldn't have mattered if you'd have been here today." She picked up a wadded paper towel from the table and rubbed it absentmindedly with her fingers.

"Rosa? Tell me what it is. I can tell you're upset."

"I was just sitting here wondering why that is," Rosa said. "Why am I so worked up over it, if they've apparently got everything worked out, Hannah and Delores? I mean, that's what we want, but something just doesn't feel right. And I'm— well, I'm worried about that darling little girl."

"What's going on with them? Did something change?"

"That's what I'm trying to figure out. Last night,

I met with Delores and talked with her about a safety plan, about what she and Hannah should do regarding her husband's abuse. I thought we'd decided that they would stay here, at least a couple more weeks, and then we'd try to approach Delores's brother. She said she has one in Mississippi and thought the two of them could go there for a while and be safe." She shrugged. "I didn't think they should go there yet, because she'd said how angry her husband would be, and I felt that there should be more time before she went somewhere that he could find her. Truthfully, I thought she should take the next steps to sever ties, because she admitted that she didn't think he'd ever stop the abuse." Rosa's mouth curved down at one edge.

"But?"

"Even though she said she shouldn't go back to him, I could see it in her eyes, hear it in her voice. That man has her soul, and she'll go back. And I'm afraid that next time, he might not stop with her."

Jenee immediately pictured the tiny little girl who'd let her read to her last night. The thought of anyone hurting Hannah…

"Let me talk to her." Even as Jenee spoke the words, she wasn't at all certain what she'd say.

"They've gone to bed, and Delores said she wasn't talking about it anymore. Trust me, I talked to her as much as anybody could."

"When are they wanting to leave?"

"Tomorrow. Her brother is picking them up at noon."

"Here? She told him where the shelter is?" Jenee asked, shocked.

"No. I was there when she called him and reminded her before I gave her the cell phone not to give out our location. They decided on a meeting place, and someone will need to drive her and Hannah to meet him there."

"I'll drive them. Where are they meeting?" Jenee asked. Maybe she could talk Delores out of leaving during the ride.

"At the fairgrounds, by the track."

"The horse track?"

"I believe that's the only place he knew of in New Orleans, which also bothers me," Rosa admitted.

"I'll take them," Jenee repeated, completely thrown by this bizarre turn of events. Delores hadn't seemed in any hurry to go, and the shelter had plenty of room. Plus, Hannah still seemed so fragile, and Jenee couldn't believe that she was ready to leave yet. She'd just started reaching out. "I don't think they need to go, not yet."

"Me neither, *chère.*" Rosa reached out and placed a hand on top of Jenee's, patting hers gently. "I haven't told you how much I appreciate you, Chantelle and Kayla bringing life back to this place again. That's what I've always wanted, to help children have a better life. I believe we're doing that. I can see how Ellie and Chylia are coming around already, and I believe Hannah would do better too, if we have the time we need to help her." She smiled. "I really do appreciate what you're doing here."

Jenee turned her hand to squeeze Rosa's palm. "I'm doing exactly what I want to do." She stood. "I'll go by their room before I go to bed."

"Okay," Rosa said, still rubbing the wadded tissue between her fingers. "Do you still have their file?"

"It's in my room."

The older lady nodded. "I may go get it, take another look to see if there's anything else I could say or do. But if Delores is determined to leave, I don't know that me saying anything about the advantages of staying here a bit longer will help."

"I'll see if she's still awake. Maybe she'll hear me out tonight if I ask her to stay for Hannah, if not for herself. That little girl isn't ready to go back, not yet. And even if they're going to her uncle's, I don't feel they'd be safe."

"I don't either, *chère,*" Rosa whispered as Jenee left the kitchen.

Delores and Hannah's room was on the other side of the shelter, and Jenee passed her own bedroom en route to theirs. Though her door was closed, she'd barely stepped in front of it before she felt a strong pull to turn and go inside. She knew that pull, knew the sensation of undiluted desire that rippled through her from that magnetism. She wasn't certain whether she was actually sensing her dream man's presence, or merely wishing that he would come to her tonight. But it took every ounce of self-control Jenee possessed to keep walking past that door knowing that he might very well be on the other side. For Hannah's sake, she had to keep Delores from making a mistake, and if the woman was still awake, Jenee needed to talk to her tonight, to hopefully get her mind entertaining the thought of staying here at least a little while longer—until Jenee believed the two of them would be safe.

With each step away from her bedroom, she felt cold, distant, lost. As though there was nothing worse than moving farther away from the possibility of being with the man she wanted so much. Jenee realized that away from him, she felt…empty. Incomplete. She barely knew him, and yet she didn't want to be without him again, ever.

By the time she reached Delores's room, her entire body ached for him, burned for him, yearned to turn around and run back to her room, and see if he was inside. But she knocked softly on the door and waited, determined that she'd talk to the woman if she could, and knowing that the minute that conversation ended, she might still go to her room and find him waiting. She had to tend to Hannah's well-being first, and then—then—she'd take care of her own needs. And do her damnedest to keep him with her this time, or at least figure out how to find him.

The door creaked as it opened, and Delores, her dark gray eyes bloodshot and swollen from sleep, peered out.

"I wanted to talk to you." Jenee found it hard to speak with all of the emotions whirling within her. Fear for Hannah, fear for Delores, desire for her dream man.

"Rosa and I already talked," Delores said, squinting now to see Jenee in the dimness of the hall light. "Hannah and I need to sleep now. We've got a big day tomorrow. Going to see my brother. Now, I appreciate everything that all of you have done to help us, but we're going where we need to go. We're doing what we need to do, and I don't want to talk no more about it."

A tiny sob echoed from the bed, and Jenee tried to look over the woman's shoulder to see Hannah.

"She's upset again," Delores said, frowning. "Just leave us be. Please. She's been through enough and needs to sleep."

"But—" was all Jenee got out before the door snapped closed.

Had Hannah been crying all day? And was Delores sure that going to her brother's place would help Hannah? Because Jenee sure wasn't.

But Jenee wasn't the little girl's mother. She'd have to keep reminding herself of that, anytime she dealt with an abused child. The court's primary goal was reunification of family, and she'd have to keep that in mind, even thought sometimes reunifying that family simply wasn't what seemed the best thing to do, particularly not when a girl was as upset as Hannah.

Jenee turned away from the door and started walking back the way she came, her steps quickening as she progressed toward her new goal. She needed to feel better now. She needed to be held. Needed someone who would understand everything she was feeling. And he would, *if* he had found his way back.

13

NICK HAD BEEN sorely tempted to go up to the attic tonight, pull out those photos and truly *see* his family again. He wished he could view them the way most family members would view pictures of lost loved ones, as a means of remembering the good times they shared and reminiscing about the past. Nick honestly didn't know if he could do that or not, view their pictures without his ability automatically kicking in and showing him the last horrible moments before they died. If he knew that he could control the visions, that he could keep their deaths at bay, then he'd waste no time retrieving the photographs and seeing them again.

But he wasn't willing to risk seeing all of them in pain.

Not for the first time, Nick despised his ability, hating what it allowed him to see, to know. However, his ability *had* helped him find children who'd been taken from their families, and it had also apparently brought him a woman who'd captured his curiosity, if not his heart.

Resisting the temptation to climb the stairs to the attic, he instead went through his bedroom to the adjoining bath. There, he took a long, hot shower, taking time to let the scalding hot water ease his tense muscles. The realization that teen prostitution was probably involved in Emma's kidnapping had both encouraged and discouraged him. Encouraged, because he had something he could work with, and he'd called Jeff immediately after leaving the hotel to have the capable staff at the center work toward finding previous hits on teen-prostitute rings in Louisiana. But discouraged, because he now knew what the couple wanted with the pretty little girl…and it made him sick.

He wouldn't allow them to keep her, to take her down that appalling road where so many girls, like the prostitute he'd spoken to at the hotel, had gone down before. Particularly when Emma hadn't gone down it willingly. It still flabbergasted Nick that the hooker had inferred that those people were actually helping those girls, but he had seen kids who were in family situations that were literally a living hell; he supposed some young girls would find having someone who promised to protect them an improvement, even if they did have to offer their bodies as part of the deal.

Nick's stomach churned. How horrible had the world become for girls to have to go through that? And how could he make it better?

Simple. One child at a time. And he'd start with Emma Moore, if he found her.

He'd finished bathing long ago, but the hot water was such a relief that he stood beneath the stream until he felt the temperature dropping. He turned off the faucet and got out, not wanting to end his day with a cold shower. Wrapping a towel around his waist, Nick moved back into his bedroom. The four-poster bed with the old-fashioned white bedspread waited for him, and he welcomed the chance to relax for a while, to ease the stress away, if only momentarily.

Nick pulled back the covers and sat on the bed, then he grabbed Emma's file from the bedside table. The worn edges on the manila folder provided yet another reminder of how many times he'd tried to connect with the child…and how many times he'd failed. He needed to see more, needed to learn more, not only to find Emma, but also to find the woman. And he only had one day left to do it.

All of his previous visions flashed before him again as he lost himself in the little girl's dark eyes. But finally, Nick saw something he hadn't seen before. The woman from the hotel fight stood nearby and reached toward Emma. She frowned, her thin lips quirked to the side, then she shook her head and reached toward Emma again. Nick watched the hand get closer, and then apparently soothe Emma's cheek. He couldn't feel it, but he could see it. The woman spoke, and Nick focused on reading her lips.

"It'll be okay. Soon. It won't be bad at all," she said, and then she smiled, but even Nick could tell that the smile was forced, and apparently, so could Emma. The vision grew blurry immediately, and Nick had no doubt she was crying.

"Where are you, *chère?*" he said, trying to capture some pertinent detail from the bedroom where the woman spoke to Emma. But, as usual, there were no details to be seen. A wooden desk, a chair with a woven cane back, the small bed Emma was resting on. No photographs on the walls, no books or maps or anything that would signal where the kidnappers were holding Emma. "Dammit," Nick growled, frustrated.

He'd barely said the words when Emma's view disintegrated, and he was, once again, standing outside of the door he knew so well. He didn't question the change of location anymore; he'd expected it. But upon entering the room, he was immediately disappointed. It was empty.

Nick surveyed the tiny bed, a plain twin bed similar to the one Emma had been sleeping on in the previous vision. It didn't have a headboard or footboard and was pushed against a corner of one wall. The old-fashioned patchwork quilt reminded him vaguely of the ones he'd seen at his grandmother's when he was a child, and was tucked neatly around the mattress. A nightstand held an antique lamp that was centered on a circle of embroidered fabric.

Nothing that would clue him in to where he was. He turned, scanned the dresser, which at first glance had nothing out of the ordinary that would help him in his quest. A hairbrush, a pink bottle of body spray, a matching bottle of lotion. He picked up the bottle, pressed the button to dispense the spray, then sniffed, hoping to capture the scent associated with his fantasy woman. The label on the bottle indicated the fragrance as Sweet Pea, but Nick smelled nothing.

Nothing. He should have known; he couldn't smell anything when he was with her; that wasn't his gift, after all. But he wanted to know how she smelled. He wanted to know lots of other things too. Wanted to hear her voice, to see her face when she'd just woken from sleep, to see her interact with children, the way she'd interacted with Emma in that book-filled room.

Nick had thought about that throughout the day today, the way she'd looked at Emma so compassionately in that vision, the way she'd smiled as though trying to convey that everything would be all right. And he now knew in his heart that she couldn't have had anything to do with the kidnapping. True, he didn't know her beyond their sexual interactions, but still…he *knew* her. Could sense her emotions, feel her excitement when she was overjoyed and her sadness when she was down. And he'd seen her when she'd looked into Emma's eyes. She cared about the girl and wanted to help her. Maybe that's what was going on, she was trying to get Emma away from the situation she was in. Maybe that's why Nick kept connecting with her, because they shared the same goal.

Then couldn't she help him find them? Couldn't she tell that he was at a dead end, and that he needed something, someone, to help him out? Hell, he'd never needed assistance on any of his former cases, but Nick knew that everything about this case was different. This time, he needed all the help he could get.

This time, he needed her.

He started to place the body spray back on the dresser, but then noticed a manila file folder, much like his own folder for Emma, underneath the small cluster of personal items on the dresser. Nick quickly moved the brush, lotion and spray to the side and opened the file.

A small photo was stapled to the inside flap and Nick immediately recognized the woman in the picture. The woman who'd been beaten at the hotel, and the same woman he'd seen with Emma in the tiny bedroom. In the photograph, her face was still beaten badly, and Nick knew that this had been taken not long after the fight, because when he'd seen her a few minutes ago in Emma's bedroom, her face had started to heal. Her eye was no longer swollen shut, as it was in this picture, and her cheek wasn't as bruised. But Nick's attention moved quickly from the woman to the little girl beside her.

The little girl with the same big dark eyes he'd seen in his own folder. He knew it was Emma. The face was identical, but different, because she was happy in the photo with her sister, and in this picture, standing beside the woman, she was sad. Her dark eyes were brimmed with tears. And her hair…was short. And black.

"Yeah, with black hair, and if she was a little older, like you said—yeah, I think that's her."

He looked at the page opposite the photo and saw a diagram labeled Violence Wheel that was divided based on physical and nonphysical forms of abuse. Tiny checkmarks had been placed in several of the spokes on the wheel, and at the bottom of the page, a single name had been written.

Delores Fosset.

He looked back at the photo. Delores Fosset. Was that the name of the woman who had taken Emma? The woman in that photo?

Noticing there were more pages in the file, he lifted the sheet with the wheel diagram and found a second page almost identical to the first, but on this graphic, different spokes were checked, and at the bottom of the page, a different name had been written.

Hannah Fosset.

Nick frowned. He'd assumed Delores Fosset was the name of the woman, but maybe her name was Hannah. Then who was Delores? He flipped the page, but there was no additional identifying information in the file; the remainder primarily dealt with abuse in general, and methods to treat victims of various forms of abuse. He turned back to the front of the file and focused on the picture. That was Emma. But…her name wasn't here.

Delores and Hannah Fosset. Two names, two violence wheels—whatever they were—and two people in the photograph. The woman, and Emma.

He ran over the details he'd assimilated over the past two weeks and thought about the couple at the hotel. None of the registered names had thrown any red flags, and Nick had surmised that was because the couple hadn't used their real names. Why would that be any different with this photo? Delores and Hannah Fosset. Chances were the adult would have been listed first, so Delores Fosset was the name the woman was using; Hannah had obviously been the name chosen for Emma.

Hannah Fosset *was* Emma Moore.

Nick was so engrossed in studying the photograph and the names that he barely registered the soft knock on the bedroom door. Only when the door actually creaked did he drop the top of the file on the dresser, which was good, since it'd have looked odd for the thing to be floating in midair when the elderly black woman opened the door.

He held his breath as she entered and wondered if she'd be able to see the guy standing near the dresser wearing nothing but a towel.

Scanning the room, she looked straight at Nick, but didn't even acknowledge his existence. Obviously, the only person that could see him this way was his woman.

His woman. How odd to think of her that way, when he barely knew her at all. But he did, and he suspected that there wasn't anything that would change that.

The elderly woman's attention landed on the file, and she moved toward it and picked it up, then opened it to look at the photograph of Emma—or Hannah—with Delores Fosset. She shook her head and frowned, then closed the file and took it with her as she left the room.

Nick watched the door close with regret. Now the file was gone. If he had it on hand, he might be able to show it to the brunette, point to Emma's photo and indicate that something was wrong. But that was no longer an option.

The door opened again, and Nick turned to see *her.* She looked at him and gave him a knowing smile, and then she locked the door.

She wore a brown T-shirt and well-worn jeans, the clothing fitting her as though it was made especially for her body, accenting her breasts, slender waist and the sweet curve of her hips. A rip above her left knee displayed a sliver of tan, toned leg, and Nick had two immediate responses to the vision before him. One, all blood had relocated south. And two, he couldn't imagine living his life without her.

She moved toward him, bringing trembling hands to his face as he pulled her close. Nick wanted her so desperately, but he also knew that their time could be extremely limited, and he had to know…

"Who is Delores Fosset?" he asked. "And Hannah? Did you know her real name is Emma? And how do you know them? Are they here, in this building? They are, aren't they?" Nick was frustrated that he couldn't control where he went in his visions. When he showed up by her door, there was only one way to go, inside. He couldn't turn and roam the place, try to find his way around and learn where he was—where Emma was. He was able to be with this incredible woman, but that was as far as he could go. Dammit, he had no idea why. If only she could tell him…

"Tell me you hear me this time, *chère,*" he said.

But as usual, she didn't hear him, or even recognize that he was trying to communicate with her. She merely looked at him as though she wanted nothing more than to stand there and gaze at him all night. "I've missed you terribly," she mouthed, and Nick couldn't do anything but nod. He'd missed her too, more than he'd even realized until now, with her where she belonged, back in his arms.

Every other time they'd been together had been wild and harried, with her particularly anxious to take them to a frantic sexual climax without an abundance of emotion along the way. Nick had wanted more every time. Yet he'd had a difficult task getting her to slow down, because apparently she was nervous someone would walk in, like the older woman had a few moments ago.

But not this time.

She eased her fingers along his jaw and toward his hair, then tunneled them through slowly, her chest rising and falling languorously as she unhurriedly touched him, rubbed against him, drew him in with her eyes.

Nick was lost to this woman, consumed by her desire, by the emotion that she conveyed with her touch. He slid his hands down her sides to the hem of her shirt and started to edge it upward, but she captured one of his hands and shook her head, then took a small step away from him. Nick let her lead the way, and when they were beside the bed, she moved her hands, still trembling, to the towel at his waist and gently tugged it free.

Her gaze moved down his chest, across his abdomen and then lingered on his erection before returning to his face. Nick didn't move. She was taking her time, learning him, enjoying the two of them together, and he didn't want to rush her, no matter how much he wanted inside of her at this very moment.

She turned back the covers and nodded toward

the bed, indicating for Nick to lie down. He did, situating himself on the pillows while she slowly pulled the shirt over her head, then dropped it to the floor.

Her bra was chocolate lace and see-through, beautifully emphasizing those sensitive little points beneath the wispy material. She slid off her shoes, then unfastened the jeans and pushed them to the floor, and Nick was greeted with matching chocolate lace panties.

She didn't remove her underwear, but climbed on the bed and straddled him, the lacy wisp of fabric between her legs rubbing teasingly against his penis. The urge to push against her heated center was so strong that Nick's breath was strained and his heart hammered against his ribs, but he wasn't going to give in to temptation. This was the first time she'd taken things slow, and Nick thought he knew why. No way in hell would he ruin what they were sharing.

Leaning over him, she brought her mouth to his forehead, nudging his hair away to kiss him at the temple, then slowly easing her lips along his jaw, and toward his ear. Her mouth was hot and wet and sweet, sucking on his lobe while her body rubbed against him, driving Nick ever so surely over the edge.

He gritted his teeth for control. She'd taken her palms to his biceps and squeezed them in an effort to keep him still, to make sure he let her have her way. Nick could easily take over, roll her on her back and show her that this slow torture could go two ways, but that wasn't what she wanted, and Nick was all about giving her everything she wanted. As much as she wanted. For as long as she wanted.

Finally her mouth found his, her tongue sliding between his lips then rubbing against his as her hips mimicked the motion, undulating slowly and fluidly. He felt her panties getting wetter, and her core getting hotter. Her heart beat violently against his chest, and Nick realized with satisfaction that she was as absorbed in this as he, and as ready as he.

She broke the kiss and moved to his neck, kissing him along the column, then biting the tender curve between his neck and shoulder.

Nick's cock lifted with that bite, and she noticed. She bit him again, and his hips lifted again, pressing his hard length against the damp heat of her panties.

The vibration against his throat was Nick's only clue that she'd moaned, or growled, or something. But whatever it was, his automatic response had taken her from slow and easy, to hard and needy. She moved her hands from his biceps, flattened them against his chest and pushed herself up, so that she was sitting on him, her center pressing mercilessly against his erection.

She reached behind her back and undid her bra, then tossed it to the side, grabbed his wrists and moved his hands to her breasts. Her head fell back and she opened her mouth in what Nick knew must have been a seductive moan. Damn, he wanted to hear it.

He kneaded her breasts until her nipples were firm, hard peaks, then he pressed them together, forcing the tips close enough that he could flick his tongue across both of them. Her head rolled from side to side wildly while her hips continued grinding against his penis, the wet lace of her panties nearly making him come from the friction alone.

Knowing that the near pain would intensify his own orgasm, he wanted to heighten her pleasure as well, and he removed his mouth from her nipples and rubbed his chin over the sensitive, wet tips. He'd shaved this morning, but hadn't shaved again before bed, and his shadowy beard provided enough friction to…

She bucked at the sensation, jerking away from his chin and then grabbing his hips to give her more control. Then she rubbed jerkily against him, and Nick could tell she was getting close, using his hard erection to stroke her clitoris to climax.

Nick had never felt so…used. And he couldn't imagine being any more pleased about it. She was enjoying herself, giving herself pleasure, and this beautiful woman letting herself go was one of the most exquisite things he'd ever seen.

Her hands tightened, gripping his hips fiercely, and her head tilted back, pushing her breasts forward, so that Nick easily captured them again and sucked one, then the other...while she came powerfully.

She trembled through the aftermath, then she looked at him, really looked at him, and gave him a soft smile. "Thank you," she mouthed, and Nick nodded, but he sure as hell hoped she didn't think this was over.

They were just getting started.

He moved his hands to her hips and lifted her away from his cock, then shifted his weight to put her on her back while he turned to his side. "My turn, *chère*."

She couldn't hear him, but her eyes said she understood, and again, she smiled.

In spite of his ready-to-plunge cock, Nick took his time, starting with soft kisses along her forehead, then across her eyes, her lashes feathering across his lips. He started kissing her cheek, but she turned her face to bring her mouth to his, and he let her have the long, lingering kiss she wanted. They didn't hurry, but enjoyed the intimacy of the kiss. He began a prolonged exploration of her mouth, sucking on her tongue, grazing her with his teeth and all the while massaging her body with his hands. Knowing they were probably still overly sensitive, he tenderly cupped her breasts, gingerly rubbing a finger across each nipple while she gasped against his lips. Then he eased his hand down her quivering abdomen to her panties.

She lifted her hips, and Nick slid the fabric down her legs, then she pushed it aside, spread her legs slightly and arched her back. She broke the kiss, looked into his eyes and mouthed, "Please."

Nick palmed her mound, her moist heat wetting his fingers. He slid one finger between her folds, then pressed it inside. His hands were big, he knew that, but she didn't back away from the invasion. Instead, her muscles clamped around him as though she'd never let him go, the same way they gripped his penis when he was inside of her.

His cock hardened to the point of pain, and pressed against her side. She twisted, trying to get it where she wanted it.

Nick withdrew the finger and slid it to her clitoris, then leisurely stroked and played with the swollen nub while she writhed against him. He massaged the sensitive spot until she shook with need, and clearly unable to wait any longer, she jerked against him, pushing her body up until the head of his penis was at her opening, and then she bit his neck. Hard.

Nick couldn't have stopped if he tried. He rammed his hips forward, territorially plowing inside of her heat, taking what he'd wanted since he arrived in this room and staking his claim. Making her his. He pumped his hips forcefully, while she continued kissing, sucking, biting his neck, joining him thrust for thrust until they both soared into mind-jarring climaxes. Nick closed his eyes, held her close and knew…the exact moment when he left her bed and returned to his own.

14

JENEE FELL into a light sleep after her dream man left, snuggling into the pillow and mattress and replaying every moment of their lovemaking in her dreams. And it *was* lovemaking. She hadn't held anything back, hadn't tried to rush toward the inevitable, hadn't tried to stop her heart from joining in the blissful, intoxicating experience. She loved him. Odd as it was, given she still hadn't spoken to the man, she loved him. And she simply had to find him, someway, somehow.

Jenee rolled onto her back and stared at the ceiling while she tried to come up with a reasonable explanation for where he was, what he was, and how to get him here permanently. She closed her eyes, thought of him pushing deep, deep within her, and the way that when they were joined everything felt so…right.

Then a familiar awareness invaded her reminiscence, and her eyes opened instantly. She knew this feeling, had experienced it sporadically since she'd turned eighteen and received her first ghostly assignment.

A soft, creamy glow formed in one corner of the tiny bedroom. The glow grew stronger and stronger, illuminating that corner as a spirit materialized before her—not her fantasy man, but a young girl.

Jenee bolted upright and blinked several times, trying to make sure she truly saw a child standing at the foot of her bed. Her hair was long and black, the same color as her onyx eyes. There was something about her, maybe the intensity of those dark eyes or perhaps the full lower lip, that reminded Jenee of someone, though she couldn't decide who.

"Are you Jenee?" the girl asked as she moved toward the bed with her head tilted, long, glowing black waves shining around her.

"I am," Jenee said, eager to learn what the little girl wanted, not only because it was her family duty to help spirits in need, but also because she knew that if this young spirit was assigned to her, then she would take priority over everything else until Jenee helped her find the light. Priority over her dream man.

"Good. Then you're the one who will help me cross over. That's what Ms. Adeline said. I've been waiting for a long while, waiting until it was the right time to help my brother, and he needs my help now. But you've got to help me tell him what to do."

"I'll help you any way I can," Jenee promised. She glanced at the antique clock on the wall of her room, noting that it was just past five in the morning. Her lover had been gone for hours, and she'd been sleeping, dreaming of him again.

"I need your help with Nick," the little girl said again. "Adeline said that I'm supposed to tell you what I need, and that's what I need. I have to help him, and it has to be today. We don't have a lot of time."

Struggling to push her own desires away long enough to help the girl, Jenee grappled with the surge of information. Usually a spirit knew nothing about the time allotted to cross; they found that out when the assigned Vicknair medium opened the letter in Grandma Adeline's sitting room. But this ghost seemed to know. How? "We don't have a lot of time?" Jenee repeated.

"No. I'm not sure how long exactly, but I do know another little girl is in danger, so don't waste time, please. It's important." And then she was gone.

In spite of the July weather, Jenee shivered. Perhaps because of the shock of receiving the spirit when she hadn't been expecting one, or perhaps it actually was a chill, since she had fallen asleep the way he'd left her, completely sated and completely naked. She moved toward the dresser to grab some clothes and saw the navy towel on the floor. Thinking of the way he had looked with this towel draped around his waist, she placed it against her cheek. Amazingly, it was still warm and it smelled… like the man she loved.

Realization slammed her hard. She had to go to the

plantation, get her assignment letter and help the child spirit. But that meant she might not make it back to the shelter before Hannah and Delores left, which meant she wouldn't get another chance to try to talk Delores into staying. And it also meant that if her dream man was actually somehow finding her *because* she was near to Hannah, then that connection would be broken. She blinked encroaching tears away—it wouldn't do any good to cry. Instead she opened one of her dresser drawers and gently laid the towel inside, next to the only other items in the drawer, the two buttons he'd left before. If she couldn't have the man, at least she'd have reminders of him.

Then Jenee shook her head as she opened another drawer and withdrew her clothes. She wouldn't think that way, not yet. There was still a chance he was alive, and she could find him. But how would she even know where to look?

"Another little girl is in danger."

Though the words were the young ghost's, the mental voice that suddenly overpowered Jenee's thoughts was that of an elderly woman. Jenee realized that she'd let her own worries take over— was Grandma Adeline giving her a nudge from the other side? She had to remember what was most important now—a child's life was at stake.

After she dressed, she hurried through the shelter to the kitchen, found a tablet and scribbled a hasty note to Rosa explaining that she had to go to the plantation. She'd call Chantelle on the way and let her know that Rosa would need her to help this morning at the shelter. Her sister-in-law wouldn't mind being awakened for this; they all knew that a ghost in need took priority over everything else. But this time, even more so, because of the ghost's warning.

"Another little girl is in danger, so don't waste time."

Jenee wouldn't waste time. Though her own heart was breaking at the possibility of losing her dream man, she wouldn't let that jeopardize a child's life. She had to help the female spirit, had to get her to her brother and save the other little girl. There was no time for self-pity now.

The Vicknair plantation was an hour away from the shelter. She drove through the darkness with fierce determination, but while the child spirit wasn't with her, Jenee let her tears fall, and didn't attempt to wipe them away. They trickled past her cheeks and down her throat as she sobbed, because she had so wished her destiny included *him.*

By the time she rounded the last curve on River Road before the plantation, Jenee had finished her solo pity party and wiped her face. The clock on her dash showed it was straight up 6:00 a.m. Hopefully, Nanette wouldn't be awake. It was Sunday, after all, and Jenee's oldest cousin typically slept late on Sunday. She turned onto the dirt road, slowed the car to ease up the driveway and at the very moment that she cleared the end of the magnolia-lined driveway, the sun rose and painted the big, white home with the first rays of morning.

Even though the house still had its share of damage from Katrina, with leaning columns and one side pressed in from the storm's force, it still took her breath away, particularly when showcased in sunlight, as it was now.

Jenee was a big believer in signs, and she prayed that the breathtaking image before her was a good sign, and that today would be a good day. How good, she didn't dare ponder. But if she saved the little girl who was in danger, that would be incredible. And if she somehow found her dream man, even better.

As if sensing her glimmer of hope, a thick cloud pushed its way in front of the golden sun, and once again, the house was veiled in shadow. It went from evoking its formidable presence from years past to something rather haunting.

Jenee parked the car and had barely climbed out before the front door to the plantation opened and Nanette, wearing a red robe and with her hair wrapped up in a towel, stepped out.

"You have a ghost here? Is it the one you've been sleeping with? I checked the tea service when I got up, but nothing was there."

Jenee sighed inwardly. So much for Nanette sleeping in. "Well, if the letter isn't there yet, it's on the way. And I still don't think he's a ghost, though I have no idea what he is. But this one isn't him, it's a little girl."

Nanette's dark brows furrowed and her mouth quirked to the side. "What happened to him?"

"I don't know."

Nan took a breath as if she was going to say more, then evidently thought better of it and snapped her mouth shut. She stepped aside as Jenee entered and started up the stairs to the sitting room.

"You, Chantelle and Celeste did a good job on the stairs," Nanette commented. "It's much safer now that they aren't all bowed up. I'm sure the committee will commend us for that."

"Thanks." Jenee didn't even look back to respond, but kept walking. She needed to help her spirit. No, not *her* spirit, but the one who needed her help today. She'd never think of any other spirit as hers again, not unless it was the one she wanted.

"Jenee?"

Nanette's tone caused Jenee to turn. "Yeah?"

"I just wanted to say that I'm sorry if he's gone."

"Yeah, me too." Jenee turned back, but still heard Nanette's mumbled words.

"Love sucks."

Jenee nearly lost her footing on the stairs as she twisted back around to ask exactly what "love" Nanette was referring to. A brief flash of her cousin and Charles Roussel against his car came to mind, but by the time Jenee steadied herself, Nanette had disappeared down the hall, probably en route to the kitchen and strong coffee.

She would definitely ask Nan about the comment later, but now there simply wasn't time. She had to get to that assignment, and help save a child.

Entering the sitting room, Jenee was immediately warmed by all of the reminders of her grandmother. Grandma Adeline had loved this room, with its big, bold pink and burgundy floral wallpaper along one wall, the red velvet settee, the grandfather clock between two elongated windows, and the coffee table that centered the entire area—not to mention the silver tea service on the coffee table. As Nanette had said, there wasn't anything on that infamous tea service where all Vicknair ghostly assignments were delivered. But by the time Jenee crossed the room and sat on the settee, a lavender envelope materialized on the shiny platter. On the outside, in her grandmother's familiar swirling script, was a single name.

Jenee.

Eager to get started, she picked up the envelope and opened it, withdrawing the usual three sheets of paper composing a medium's assignment. The top one, pale purple stationery with a scalloped border, carried Adeline Vicknair's trademark scent, magnolia. Jenee read the information at the top of the page.

Name of Deceased—Sophie Madere.

The name didn't spark any recognition. Jenee didn't recall hearing the name on the news or reading anything about the child in the paper, so she wondered if she wasn't from around here, and whether this assignment might require Jenee to travel, away from the plantation and away from the shelter…the only place where she'd been able to see her dream man. Then again, she suspected she wouldn't see him again anyway if Hannah left.

She swallowed, then continued reading. The center section of her grandmother's letter confirmed the reason for death.

Reason for Death—Drowned during Hurricane Katrina.

Jenee reread the single line. During Hurricane Katrina? The girl had been dead for three years? Why hadn't she crossed? She'd said she needed to get to her brother. Had he survived? Yes, he must have, because she said she had to get to him to save another little girl.

The bottom of the page verified what Jenee suspected.

Requirement for Passage—Helping her brother accept his destiny and save Emma Moore.

"His destiny?" That sounded so much like the Vicknairs—in fact it was the very way they described their unique ability to communicate with ghosts that were stuck in the middle. It was their "destiny." What kind of destiny did Sophie Madere's brother have?

She flipped the purple page over and dropped it on the settee, then moved to the second sheet. As usual, it listed rules for dealing with the spirits. Jenee knew them all, but she was required to read the pages in their entirety before an assignment officially began. Then she tossed the sheet of rules to the side so she could view the final page, the official document directing her grandmother to assign Sophie Madere to one of her grandchildren.

> *TO: Adeline Vicknair, Grand Matriarch of Vicknair Mediums*
> *FROM: Lionelle Dewberry, Gatekeeper First Class*
> *CC: Board of Directors, Realm Entrance Governing Squadron*
> *SUBJECT: Case # 19-46-1921—Sophie Madere*
> *Current Status—Access Pending*
> *Required Rectification—Ensuring that Nick Madere saves Emma Moore and accepts his destiny*
> *Time Allotted for Rectification—Four hours*

Four hours? "Hours?" Jenee had no idea where this Nick Madere was, or what would be involved in helping him save a little girl—four hours couldn't be long enough.

"Come on. We don't have time to waste. That

girl's life depends on us, and on my brother." Sophie Madere was tiny, and no more than eight or nine years old, yet she stood at the doorway, her brows arched imperiously, waiting for Jenee to heed her summons. "Come on. You have to come," she repeated insistently, and Jenee knew better than to question the impatient spirit. They didn't have time for answers.

The paper in her hand disintegrated, and Jenee hurried toward the door. "Where are we going?"

"My brother's home in New Orleans. That's where he is now, so that's where we have to go. And we have to hurry, so drive fast. Please."

Jenee hurried after the girl and yelled to Nanette that she was leaving without waiting for her cousin to respond. She ran to her car and climbed in, while Sophie Madere moved through the door and sat in the passenger's seat. Jenee started the engine, then sped down the driveway without looking back. The sun was in full force now, making her squint as she drove, but she wouldn't slow down. She had four hours to do…whatever they needed to do. "What's the address?"

"It's 455 Orange Street. It's in the Garden District."

"Yes, I know—"

"Good," the girl said, again sounding much older than she looked. "We need to hurry. We can't waste time. He needs your help." She paused, then said, "He needs you."

15

NICK WAS ON HIS fourth pot of coffee. He'd had less than an hour of sleep, but he had to concentrate on what he'd learned when he connected to Emma.

Emma Moore was Hannah Fosset, and Hannah Fosset was with Delores Fosset, and both of them were with his fantasy woman. He'd been on and off the phone with Jeff Stewart throughout the night and had an entire team at the center trying to find information on the name or pseudonym Delores Fosset, as well as any information they could about teen prostitution in Louisiana and the surrounding states. So far, they'd located seven women named Delores Fosset in the States, but hell, it could be a case of identity theft, for all Nick knew, with this "Fosset" lady stealing someone else's identity in the course of running the prostitution ring.

Or, there was the off chance that one of the Delores Fossets listed was actually the woman Nick had seen in the photograph and in his visions.

He clicked the mouse on his computer again, taking another look at the mug shots Jeff had sent.

Three of the seven women had a criminal history, and wouldn't you know—none of them matched the woman Nick had seen.

Of the remaining four, only one lived in the Southeast, in Picayune, Mississippi. That was close enough to New Orleans to warrant more interest. He'd called the number listed for her but didn't get an answer.

Nick stared at Emma's photograph again. Ever since he'd left his lady last night, he hadn't been able to see anything new when he connected with Emma. He could repeat the previous visions, but no new clues were revealed, and even with the names he'd found, he didn't know which way to go, what to do.

The high-pitched chimes of his doorbell invaded the home. Still pondering what he should do next, he went to the front door, opened it—and saw *her*. His fantasy woman stood before him. Nick had to touch her, had to verify that this was real, that she was real.

"You're here? You're Nick Madere?" she questioned, those beautiful brown eyes he loved so much glistening as she reached for him. Their arms circled each other, and he pulled her close, so close, but still not close enough. "I thought I'd lost you," she said. "I didn't think you had crossed, but I didn't know how to find you either."

"Crossed?" Nick had no idea what she was

talking about, but he didn't care. She was here, not in a dream or in a fantasy or whatever the hell he wanted to call it, and she spoke, and he *heard* her.

She *was* here. In his arms, in his life, and he never intended to let her go. He cupped her face in his hands, welcoming the softness of her skin, the familiarity of her body. He knew her so well, and yet he didn't know her at all…but he would.

He didn't care that they were standing in his doorway and that he should be asking her how she'd gotten here, or why. He wanted his mouth on hers.

Her lips parted and she accepted his kiss with a low, keening moan that vibrated against his mouth. Then she tunneled her fingers through his hair and pressed her lips hard against his, eager to give as much as she took, so that this kiss, and this moment, would last forever.

A coughing fit followed by soft laughter was the first thing Nick heard, and he and his woman— hell, he still didn't know her name—broke their kiss to see an elderly lady walking a couple of poodles, but currently more interested in the activities occurring on his porch.

Nick nodded at the lady, then pulled *his* lady inside the house and shut the door.

"Tell me your name," he said.

"Jenee. Jenee Vicknair," she said breathlessly, her mouth reddened from the pressure of his lips. He hoped to make her mouth that red again, daily, hourly.

"Jenee," he repeated, trying out the name and realizing that it was perfect. Feminine. Desirable. Sexy. *Jenee.*

His Jenee.

"There's so much I need to know about you." He wanted to learn her likes, her dislikes, where she came from, how she'd connected with him, but he didn't get to ask specifics before she spoke again— and her words blew him away.

"I have someone with me," she said. "Or rather, her spirit is here. I know this will be hard to understand, and I usually try to take more time to explain, but we don't have time. Sophie is with me. Your sister's spirit is here, with me—and she says we have to hurry."

"Sophie?" Nick questioned, but then he felt a sensation, like someone—his beloved little sister— had hugged him. "Sophie's here?"

"Yes," Jenee said, sounding relieved that he hadn't called her crazy. "And she says there's no time for explaining all of this right now. We all need to work together to find a little girl who is in trouble." She paused. "Emma Moore. Do you know Emma Moore?"

"She's the reason I'm here," he told her, still overwhelmed at the idea of his sister being there, and that his mystery woman, Jenee, was too.

"Who is she? Where is she?" Jenee asked anxiously. "We have to find her soon."

"I believe you know her too," Nick said, "as Hannah Fosset."

Her dark eyes grew wide. "Hannah?"

Nick's emotions were at an all-time high. He'd found the woman he wanted, or rather, she'd found him. And now he realized that he was on the brink of finding Emma. But before he could even ask where she was, words tumbled out of Jenee's mouth.

"Sophie is about to cross over," she said. "That was what she stayed in the middle for. She had to make sure that the two of us got together to save Emma—Hannah. She said now it's up to us."

Nick just looked at her, trying to grasp the flurry of information that had hit him all at once. This woman, Jenee Vicknair, claimed to communicate with his sister, who was dead. Not only that, but she knew what Sophie wanted and apparently knew something about "the other side."

Jenee looked up at him as though knowing exactly what he was thinking, wondering. But why wouldn't she? They'd shared so much, shared their bodies without their names, and shared their emotions without their words. They'd become one, in several senses of the word, and he still felt that way with her now. He knew she'd tell him what he wanted to know without him even having to ask.

"I'm a medium. I help ghosts cross over when they're in the middle realm and can't find their way.

Or, in Sophie's case, when they have something they want to accomplish before they cross. She wanted you to remember your past and accept your ability. And she says you don't *have* to see anything you don't want to see."

"I can control it, you mean," he said, understanding completely. Their photographs. He could look at his family's photographs and actually reminisce about the past, about the good times, instead of seeing their last moments.

Jenee nodded, but not toward Nick. She was obviously listening to Sophie, and Nick wasn't about to interrupt her.

When she finally looked up again, she added, "Sophie says it's up to you. You *can* see everything that happened that day, but you don't have to." Jenee smiled, apparently to his little sister. "And Sophie recommends you not try, because none of that matters anymore. They're all in a terrific place now, so why don't you just remember the good times and not look for the bad." This time, Jenee smiled at Nick. "Your sister is quite intelligent for such a little girl."

"Eight going on twenty," he said, returning her smile. "That's what I always said about you, Sophie, wasn't it?"

"She's smiling and nodding," Jenee told him.

"Had a feeling she was. Sophie," Nick then whispered, crouching down the way he used to when he wanted to talk eye level to his sister. The moment he got there, he sensed a tiny pressure on his right cheek. He moved his hand to the spot.

"She wanted to kiss you bye," Jenee confirmed, and Nick's throat tightened with emotion. "And she says she's leaving because it isn't her place to help you find Emma now. She's done what she was supposed to do—tell you to accept your ability and not be afraid of the photos, and get the two of us together so we can help Emma—Hannah."

"I love you, Sophie." Nick knew the moment she left. He didn't understand how, but he knew. Something about the very air around him changed, and he felt a sudden awareness of being alone. Then he stood and looked at Jenee.

"I'm not going anywhere," she whispered, knowing his thoughts before he even expressed them. "Ever."

"Neither am I, but we have to find Emma first."

"And Emma, the girl you're looking for, is Hannah?" she questioned, confusion etched plainly on her face. "But Hannah came to the shelter with her mother, Delores Fosset."

The shelter. That's where they were in Nick's visions, a shelter. The pieces started falling into place. Delores Fosset had taken Emma to a place that would not only protect them, but also ask no questions about her bruises or Emma's upset state. A shelter for battered women. No wonder his brunette beauty—Jenee—had looked so compassionate toward Emma. She was taking care of her.

Nick wrapped one arm around her as he guided her toward the table and the opened file.

"Oh, my, it is Hannah." She reached for the photo, then lifted it for a better view. "Her hair…"

"I'm guessing they cut it and dyed it," Nick said.

"Is that her sister?" Jenee asked, pointing to Maggie, a smaller, brown-haired version of Emma.

"Yes, that's her sister, Maggie. She was with Emma and their mother at a park in Atlanta when the kidnappers got Emma."

"Oh, Hannah, bless her little heart." She gasped softly. "No wonder she was upset when I read her that book. She *doesn't* look like the girl on the cover."

Nick knew they didn't have time for her to explain, so he didn't ask. Instead, he went straight to what was important. "Where are they? Where is the shelter? Are they still there?"

"They were planning to leave later this morning, but I'll call Rosa and make sure that they haven't gone," Jenee said, withdrawing a cell phone from her pocket. She explained as she dialed, "Rosa is the woman overseeing the shelter. It's called the Seven Sisters, a place for women and children who've been abused."

Nick nodded, his previous suspicion authenticated. The woman, Delores Fosset, if that was her real name, was smarter than he'd realized. No wonder there were no markings on the building in his vision; an abuse shelter wouldn't have any identifying features, since its location was meant to be confidential. It all made sense now.

While Jenee spoke to Rosa, Nick leaned closer to Emma's picture. "Show me something, Emma. Where are you now?"

The images sped through Nick's mind in strobelight fashion, flashing through the car ride, the swamp, the hotel and then the building—what Nick now knew was the Seven Sisters shelter.

Then a new image pushed ahead of the others. Horses. Barn stalls. And a big, bold, red-and-blue sign that told Nick exactly what he needed to know, where Emma was now. At least, he sure hoped she was still there and this wasn't merely a memory. It couldn't be. He had to find her, had to save her.

"She's at the fairgrounds, in the paddock. She's scanning the crowd as though she's looking for someone, or maybe as though she's scared she's going to see someone," he said, processing the information as he relayed it to Jenee.

"How do you know that?" Jenee asked, snapping her phone closed.

"*That's* my ability, or blessing, or whatever you want to call it. I see through others' eyes." He tapped the photo. "Using their photograph. I'll explain more later, when we have time. Was that Rosa you were talking to? What did she say?" Grabbing

Emma's file in one hand and taking Jenee's hand in the other, he quickly led her out of the house. "Come on, tell me as we go. I get the feeling we don't have as much time as we'd like." They exited the house and sprinted toward his car.

"She said that they left thirty minutes ago with Chantelle, my sister-in-law, taking them to the fairgrounds. I was supposed to take them, but Delores didn't want to wait. Rosa said Delores got anxious to go, saying her brother usually gets places really early, and she didn't want to upset him by not being there when he arrived." She took a quick breath and continued, "I don't think it's her brother. I'm afraid it might be her husband she's meeting, the man who beat her and the one who Hannah is scared of. I thought he was her father, but now I know she's scared because he took her from her family. We can't let him get to them, Nick."

There was something very gratifying about hearing his dream woman say his name. Unfortunately, he couldn't truly appreciate it now, because they had to get to that little girl, and quick. Nick unlocked the car doors and climbed in. "I need to call the police."

"I asked Rosa to call them and to tell them to get to the fairgrounds. I'm sure she's already filled them in, but I wonder if they'll get there in time, if Delores's husband is there already. How far is it from here?" Jenee asked, climbing in beside him as though this was totally normal, the two of them together, helping each other to find a missing child. He realized how very natural it felt.

"I'm thinking twenty minutes."

"I hope that's soon enough."

"It has to be," Nick said, pulling out of his driveway and making a beeline through the Garden District for the fairgrounds…and Emma.

Jenee should've been watching the road ahead, the streets that rapidly changed as they worked their way toward the fairgrounds and Hannah. But watching wouldn't make them get there any quicker, and meant she'd have to take her eyes off him.

Nick Madere.

His name suited him, the strength of his features, that strong jaw set and determined, that familiar five o'clock shadow a little more intense in the morning, showing he hadn't shaved since last night…when he'd rubbed that beautiful face across her breasts until she'd squirmed wildly and then came violently.

She'd thought she'd never see him again, thought she'd never learn how he came to her, and what part Hannah had played in his arrival in Jenee's life. Now she knew: he'd connected with her because of what she was, a medium. And she'd connected with him because of what he was, a psychic.

They were both unique, both intent on fulfilling

their destinies. But now…beginning with Hannah—Emma—they could fulfill those destinies together. As one. She'd meant what she told him earlier. She wasn't going anywhere, ever. And neither was he. She could sense it in the way he held her, the way he kissed her, the way that, even now, when driving through New Orleans at breakneck speed, he'd reached for her hand and placed it on his thigh, as though he simply needed her to touch him, to prove that she was here, where he wanted her to be. Where she wanted to be.

Nick increased the car's speed as they approached the fairgrounds. He jerked the steering wheel to turn toward the paddocks; his tires squealed loudly, and the scent of burnt rubber filled the interior of the car.

Jenee hurriedly scanned the area and spotted Delores, pulling Hannah steadily along beside her as she walked purposefully toward a big man. "Nick, hurry! There they are!"

"I know. I see." He swore. Just then two police cars with lights flashing and sirens blasting entered the parking area from the rear exits, and the man near Delores and Hannah turned quickly toward the sound of the sirens, then lunged for the woman and the girl. He grabbed Delores, who frantically reached for Hannah. The man reached toward the top of his jeans, and Jenee saw a handle protruding out of his waist. He had a gun, and his focus was centered on Hannah…

Jenee grabbed the door handle and yanked it, then fell out of the car as Nick stomped the brake and skidded to a stop. "Hannah!" The name tore from her throat as she tried to get the girl to move out of Delores's reach, to get away from the two before the man had a chance to use the gun.

"Jenee! Emma!" Nick bellowed their names from behind her. Jenee heard his footsteps, knew he was near, but she couldn't stop. Hannah was terrified, trembling and crying, and Delores was grabbing for her. And the man—he was also reaching toward her with one hand, and with the other…

"Hannah, get away from them!" Jenee yelled, the words almost strangling in her throat from her fear.

Hannah's eyes widened as she recognized Jenee, then she turned away—at the precise moment that the gun went off. Delores threw up her hand defensively, and the bullet sailed through her palm, then barely missed Hannah's head. Delores's bloodcurdling scream echoed loudly from where the three stood.

But the man wasn't finished, and he turned, his eyes glaring with anger, toward…Jenee. He raised the gun, pointed the barrel directly at her—and fired.

Everything slowed to a crawl: the deafening sound of the bullet leaving the chamber, the realization that it was aimed at her, the panic that Hannah wouldn't be safe, the regret that she could have had the man that she'd always wanted, but she wouldn't. *Everything* slowed, everything twisted, everything

came to a blistering, blinding white pinnacle…then
the man that she'd finally found, the man she loved,
hurled his body in front of hers.

"No!"

16

THOUGH THE SOUND was muted on the television, Jenee watched yet another broadcast of Emma Moore's parents hugging their daughters tightly. She didn't need to hear a thing to see that all was right again in their world, their tears of gratitude and smiles of joy said more than any words could.

She twisted in the uncomfortable chair and looked at the man sleeping in the hospital bed. Nick's shoulder was bandaged and would take time to heal from the bullet wound, but according to the doctors, there would be no permanent damage, thank God. He'd saved Emma Moore, and he'd saved Jenee too, taking the bullet that was meant for her.

She eased toward the bed, not wanting to wake him but needing to be closer, and looked at the face that had been constantly in her thoughts since he'd first arrived in her dreams, a face she never wanted to be away from again. He'd wakened earlier asking for a shower, and the nurse had said no, to which he'd scowled, then smiled at Jenee and said something to the effect that she could sponge bath him later, then had drifted back into his drug-induced sleep while she'd laughed. There was so much they had to talk about, but they could wait. They had their whole lives, after all.

It'd been nearly two days since they'd found Hannah—Emma—at the fair grounds. In that brief time, the Fossets—their real names, after all—had been charged with kidnapping and attempted murder, not to mention additional charges that stemmed from their prostitution ring, and her cousin Gage, and several other capable doctors at Ochsner Hospital, had taken care of the man she loved.

Quite a lot for a two-day period.

Jenee had only left the hospital once, earlier today, to retrieve a stack of family photographs from Nick's attic. After explaining to her why he'd been afraid to view the only pictures he had left of them and that Sophie's message had told him he didn't *have* to see them in pain, he'd asked Jenee to get them. She had, and then she'd been blessed to watch the big, beautiful man tremble with emotion as he reminisced about the good times they'd shared. Granted, the reminiscence was a bit broken and in-coherent at times, given his pain medication, but that only made Jenee appreciate him sharing them all the more. He hadn't wanted to wait any longer to see those pictures, which spoke volumes about the man she loved. Family was important to him, just like her family was important to her.

And speaking of her family, the majority of the Vicknair clan had been around Nick's room at all times, making communicating difficult, particularly when Tristan was around. Turned out that her big brother was a fan of the LSU defensive back who had dominated the football field eight years ago. Jenee had now heard all about the great Nick Madere and all the records he held. She grinned. If she'd have paid more attention to Tristan's football fixation back then, maybe she'd have recognized Nick when he came to her in her dreams.

In any case, he was here now, and he'd saved her, putting her life before his when Marcus Fosset had pulled the trigger.

Her lip trembled. The thought of what could have happened to him…

"Hey now, don't start that again. I don't want a weeping girl, you know."

She hadn't even realized her attention had moved from his face to his hand, clasping her own even as he'd slept. Now she looked up into those incredible turquoise eyes and saw a love like she'd never known, until now. "You're awake," she said, her mouth quickly curving into a smile.

"Yeah, and you're feeling guilty again. This wasn't your fault, *chère*." He indicated his shoulder. "It's Marcus Fosset's fault. And hell, it isn't much more than a scratch. Like the doctor said, I'll be good as new in no time. And we found her, didn't we?"

"But I nearly got you killed in the process."

"No, you nearly got *yourself* killed in the process, and I'm just glad I was able to keep that from happening. We're just getting started, *chère*. We can't stop now."

A soft knock sounded, then the door creaked open and Jenee's brother poked his head in.

"Oh, good, you're awake," Tristan said. "Up for company?"

Nick grinned. "Of course."

Thanks to the Vicknair cousins, his room was probably the most heavily trafficked place in the hospital, and it'd been even more so Sunday night, when Emma's family had visited Nick to thank him, and the media had perched directly outside to broadcast what they could of the event.

Tristan entered and was followed by Chantelle, who was then followed by Gage and Kayla, Dax and Celeste, and finally Monique and Ryan.

Jenee shook her head and shrugged. "Here comes my family to take over again."

Nick squeezed her hand. "I like your family, very much." He'd spent most of his waking hours over the past day visiting with them, getting to know more about each of them and the Vicknair history in general, and she'd done the same, learning from Nick about the family he'd lost—his parents, Luc and Amelie Madere, and Sophie, the sister who'd brought them together and had helped them save

Emma. He'd had some story to tell about each family photo, and Jenee had absorbed them all, wanting to learn as much as she could about the people he'd loved so much.

"How's the arm?" Tristan asked. "You aren't a leftie, are you?"

"No," Nick said, lifting the hand clasping Jenee's, "I'm a rightie."

Tristan nodded. "Good thing. You'll still be able to sign autographs then."

Nick smirked. "Haven't had a lot of people asking for those."

"With all of those records you set at LSU? Hell, I just knew you'd go pro."

"I believe all of those records have been broken, a few times now. And my life took another direction." He looked at Jenee and winked. "And I wouldn't trade this direction for anything."

Chantelle punched her husband. "Okay, Tristan, enough football talk today. You've badgered him nonstop ever since you learned who he was."

Tristan smiled broadly. "Well, shit, if I'd have known last week that Jenee was talking about Nick Madere when she was at the house…"

Chantelle's brows lifted. "You wouldn't have had a problem with your sister sleeping with a ghost if you'd have known that the ghost was a football star? Somehow, I'm having to question your reasoning on that one."

Nick cleared his throat. "For the record, I'm not a ghost, thank God." Then he shot another look at Jenee. "You told them we were sleeping together?"

"It kind of slipped out," she said, "and I sure didn't expect anyone to mention it."

She glanced pointedly at Chantelle, who put a hand over her mouth and mumbled, "Sorry, Jenee."

Jenee laughed. "No problem. Technically, I don't think we've slept together, since it was pretty much only in our minds, right?" she asked Nick.

"Trust me, *chère,* we did." His blue eyes smoldered, and Jenee felt her insides quiver.

"O-kay," Monique said. "I think that's probably all the information we need for now."

Gage and Dax turned toward her, and Gage said what they all were thinking. "Is that my sister squelching a conversation about sex?"

Monique giggled and rubbed a hand over her swollen belly. "Must be the hormones. But I do think this conversation is probably one that should be reserved for the two of them, alone. And now that Nick is awake, we should give them some time like that, alone." She stepped toward the bed, placing a hand on Jenee's shoulder. "We just wanted to stop by and see you, let you know that we're still thinking about you."

Jenee noticed that one Vicknair was missing from the room. "What about Nanette?"

"The inspection was this morning," Tristan said.

"It went fine, but evidently Roussel has put pressure on the society to make a definite decision about the place by next month, and they've agreed to. The two of them had words, and she's got it in her head that they're going to tear the plantation down."

"What do you think?" Jenee asked.

"Hard to tell. They were impressed with our efforts, but pointed out that hurricane season repeats itself every September, and they didn't know if the place could handle another severe storm. They also didn't know if they wanted to put the money into it that it'd take to ensure that it did."

"So Nanette is…" Jenee prompted.

"She's fuming and planning," Dax said. "But Celeste and I are heading back over there to calm her down and help her figure out what we need to do over the next few weeks to have a better chance of getting the answer we want."

Jenee nodded. "Count me in to help."

"Rosa scheduled additional volunteers for the shelter over the next few weeks, so that we can spend more time at the house when we're needed," Chantelle told her.

"I'll help too," Nick said from the bed. Before Jenee could argue with him on it, he added, "I'll be good as new soon, and I'm damn good with a hammer. And I don't need my left shoulder for it, since, as Tristan pointed out, I'm a rightie."

"Don't worry, Jenee," Gage said. "We won't

release him from the hospital until he's ready to go."
Then he said to Nick, "And whenever you are at the
house, I'll make sure I'm there too."

"How about that, my own personal physician,"
Nick grumbled, but he smiled with the words and
Gage returned the grin.

One by one, the Vicknair clan said their good-
byes and left. Finally, Jenee had him to herself.

"Hey, you," he said, releasing her hand and then
touching a finger to her mouth. "There's something
I've been wanting to tell you."

She had a good idea what that was, and she'd
been waiting for the right moment too. "What a co-
incidence." Her mouth moved against his finger as
she spoke. "There's something I've been wanting to
tell you also."

Then the door, once again, creaked open, and a
nurse came in to check Nick's blood pressure.

"We'll finish this conversation in a second." Nick
sounded frustrated and Jenee smiled.

She wanted to tell him she loved him, and she
would. But what did the future hold? Nick's job
was in Virginia, away from New Orleans, and
away from Jenee. And she couldn't very well leave
Louisiana when all of her ghostly assignments
came via her grandmother's sitting room at the
plantation. Plus, there was the shelter to think
about, and all of her plans to help abused girls
there. That had always been her goal, her dream.

But now she had a bigger dream—one that included Nick Madere.

As she pondered the possibilities, the nurse left, and Nick zoned in on her very thoughts. "I need to tell you about something that happened this morning," he said. "With all of the media attention I've been getting, the police department here noticed. While you were gone to my house for those pictures, they came by asking if I'd be interested in taking on a position at the local level. I'd still help with locating missing children, but I'd be involved in all missing person's cases, not just juvenile investigations."

"And?" Jenee asked hopefully.

He smiled. "And I took the job."

"You took the job," she repeated, her pulse skittering wildly. He was moving back here, back to the place that'd been his home and back to a place where they could build their future together.

"So," he continued, "I mentioned I had something to tell you." He took a deep breath, let it out slow, then said the words she'd been waiting to hear for what seemed like a lifetime. "Jenee Vicknair, I love you."

Her heart swelling and her entire body trembling with the knowledge that he was here, and he was hers, and that he would be hers forever, she leaned over the bed, kissed him softly and whispered, "I love you."

He laughed. "I know this is going to seem a little sudden, given we only started speaking two days ago, but, Jenee Vicknair, *chère,* will you marry me?

I can't get down on one knee at the moment, but the sentiment is still the same."

"You know, when you marry a Vicknair, you actually inherit the Vicknair ability to help lost ghosts find their way," she said.

Those turquoise eyes sparkled, and his gorgeous smile crept into his cheeks. "Then let me rephrase the question." He cleared his throat dramatically. "Jenee Vicknair, will you marry me, put up with my uncanny ability to see the world through someone else's eyes—and allow me to be a medium too, since two *blessings* are bound to be better than one?"

She laughed, laughed until her stomach hurt, until her tears fell, and until she had him laughing also. "Yes, Nick Madere, I'll marry you, put up with your ability…and give you mine, if you want me enough to take it."

"Trust me, *chère,* I do."

He kissed her, an intense, intimate kiss that made her shiver to her toes. Then, trailing a fingertip along the side of her face, he said, "We've still got a lot to learn about each other, don't we?"

She nodded, every dream she'd ever had becoming a reality in this moment. "No problem. We have an entire lifetime."

SPECIAL EDITION™

NEW YORK TIMES
BESTSELLING AUTHOR

DIANA PALMER

A brand-new Long, Tall Texans novel

HEART OF STONE

Feeling unwanted and unloved, Keely returns
to Jacobsville and to Boone Sinclair, a rancher
troubled by his own past. Boone has always
seemed reserved, but now Keely discovers a
sensuality with him that quickly turns to love. Can
they each see past their own scars to let love in?

*Available September 2008
wherever you buy books.*

SPECIAL EDITION

A late-night walk on the beach resulted
in Trevor Marlowe's heroic rescue of a
drowning woman. He took the amnesia
victim in and dubbed her Venus, for the
goddess who'd emerged from the sea.
It looked as if she might be his goddess of
love, too...until her former fiancé showed
up on Trevor's doorstep.

Don't miss

THE BRIDE WITH NO NAME

by *USA TODAY* bestselling author
MARIE FERRARELLA

*Available August
wherever you buy books.*

Harlequin® Historical
Historical Romantic Adventure!

From *USA TODAY*
bestselling author
Margaret Moore

A LOVER'S KISS

A Frenchwoman in London,
Juliette Bergerine is unexpectedly
thrown together in hiding with
Sir Douglas Drury. As lust and
desire give way to deeper emotions,
how will Juliette react on discovering
that her brother was murdered—
by Drury!

*Available September
wherever you buy books.*

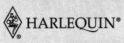

HARLEQUIN®

American ★ Romance®

Marin Thomas
A Coal Miner's Wife
Hearts of Appalachia

High-school dropout and recently widowed
Annie McKee has twin boys to raise. The
now single mom is torn between choosing
charity from her Appalachian clan or leaving
Heather's Hollow and finding a better future
for her boys. But her handsome neighbor and
deceased husband's best friend is determined
to show the proud widow there's nothing
secondhand about love!

***Available August
wherever books are sold.***

LOVE, HOME & HAPPINESS

REQUEST YOUR FREE BOOKS!

2 FREE NOVELS PLUS 2 FREE GIFTS!

◈ HARLEQUIN®

Blaze™

Red-hot reads!

YES! Please send me 2 FREE Harlequin® Blaze™ novels and my 2 FREE gifts (gifts are worth about $10). After receiving them, if I don't wish to receive any more books, I can return the shipping statement marked "cancel". If I don't cancel, I will receive 6 brand-new novels every month and be billed just $4.24 per book in the U.S. or $4.71 per book in Canada, plus 25¢ shipping and handling per book and applicable taxes, if any*. That's a savings of 15% or more off the cover price! I understand that accepting the 2 free books and gifts places me under no obligation to buy anything. I can always return a shipment and cancel at any time. Even if I never buy another book, the two free books and gifts are mine to keep forever.

151 HDN ERVA   351 HDN ERUX

Name _____ (PLEASE PRINT)

Address _____ Apt. #

City _____ State/Prov. _____ Zip/Postal Code

Signature (if under 18, a parent or guardian must sign)

Mail to the **Harlequin Reader Service:**
IN U.S.A.: P.O. Box 1867, Buffalo, NY 14240-1867
IN CANADA: P.O. Box 609, Fort Erie, Ontario L2A 5X3

Not valid to current subscribers of Harlequin Blaze books.

Want to try two free books from another line?
Call 1-800-873-8635 or visit www.morefreebooks.com.

* Terms and prices subject to change without notice. N.Y. residents add applicable sales tax. Canadian residents will be charged applicable provincial taxes and GST. Offer not valid in Quebec. This offer is limited to one order per household. All orders subject to approval. Credit or debit balances in a customer's account(s) may be offset by any other outstanding balance owed by or to the customer. Please allow 4 to 6 weeks for delivery. Offer available while quantities last.

Your Privacy: Harlequin Books is committed to protecting your privacy. Our Privacy Policy is available online at www.eHarlequin.com or upon request from the Reader Service. From time to time we make our lists of customers available to reputable third parties who may have a product or service of interest to you. If you would prefer we not share your name and address, please check here. ☐

HB08R

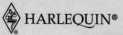 HARLEQUIN®

 *Blaze™*

COMING NEXT MONTH

#411 SECRET SEDUCTION Lori Wilde
Perfect Anatomy, Bk. 2
Security specialist Tanner Doyle is an undercover bodyguard protecting surgeon
Vanessa Rodriguez at the posh Confidential Rejuvenations clinic. Luckily,
keeping the good doctor close to his side won't be a problem—the sizzling
sexual chemistry between them is like a fever neither can escape....

#412 THE HELL-RAISER Rhonda Nelson
Men Out of Uniform, Bk. 5
After months of wrangling with her greedy stepmother over her inheritance, the
last thing Sarah Jane Walker needs is P.I. Mick Chivers reporting on her every
move. Although with sexy Mick around, she's tempted to give him something
worth watching....

#413 LIE WITH ME Cara Summers
Lust in Translation
Philly Angelis has been in love with Roman Oliver forever, but he's always treated
her like a kid. But not for long... Philly's embarking on a trip to Greece—to find her
inner Aphrodite! And heaven help Roman when he catches up with her....

#414 PLEASURE TO THE MAX! Cami Dalton
Cassie Parker gave up believing in fairy tales years ago. So when her aunt
sends her a gift—a lover's box, reputed to be able to make fantasies come
true—Cassie's not impressed...until a sexy stranger shows up and seduces
her on the spot. Now she's starring in an X-rated fairy tale of her very own.

#415 WHISPERS IN THE DARK Kira Sinclair
Radio talk show host Christopher Faulkner, aka Dr. Desire, has been helping
people with their sexual hang-ups for years. But when he gets an over-the-air
call from vulnerable Karyn Mitchell, he suspects he'll soon be the one in over
his head....

#416 FLASHBACK Jill Shalvis
American Heroes: The Firefighters, Bk. 2
Firefighter Aidan Donnelly has always battled flames with trademark icy calm.
That is, until a blazing old flame returns—in the shape of sizzling soap star
Mackenzie Stafford! Aidan wants to pour water over the unquenchable heat
between them. But that just creates more steam....

HBCNM0708